A STUDY GUIDE AND N

THE
WESTERN
EXPERIENCE

VOLUME I
TO THE EIGHTEENTH CENTURY

A STUDY GUIDE AND MAP SUPPLEMENT FOR

THE
WESTERN
EXPERIENCE

VOLUME I
TO THE EIGHTEENTH CENTURY
SIXTH EDITION

Mortimer Chambers
University of California, Los Angeles
Raymond Grew
University of Michigan
David Herlihy
Late of Brown University
Theodore K. Rabb
Princeton University
Isser Woloch
Columbia University

Prepared by
Dennis Sherman
John Jay College of Criminal Justice
City University of New York

McGraw-Hill, Inc.
New York   St. Louis   San Francisco   Auckland   Bogotá
Caracas   Lisbon   London   Madrid   Mexico City   Milan
Montreal   New Delhi   San Juan   Singapore
Sydney   Tokyo   Toronto

To Marvin, Eva, Raymond, and Pat

A Study Guide and Map Supplement for
THE WESTERN EXPERIENCE
Volume I: To the Eighteenth Century

This book is printed on acid-free paper.

2 3 4 5 6 7 8 9 0 DOC DOC 9 0 9 8 7 6

ISBN 0-07-011073-5

This book was set in Sabon by Ann Eisner/Paula Martin.
The editors were Nancy Blaine, Ira C. Roberts, and Paul R. Sobel;
the production supervisor was Kathryn Porzio.
The cover was designed by Wanda Lubelska.
R. R. Donnelley & Sons Company was printer and binder.

ABOUT THE AUTHOR

Dennis Sherman is Professor of History at John Jay College of Criminal Justice, the City University of New York. He received his B.A. (1962) and J.D. (1965) from the University of California at Berkeley and his Ph.D. (1970) from the University of Michigan. He was Visiting Professor at the University of Paris (1978–1979; 1985). He received the Ford Foundation Prize Fellowship (1968–1969, 1969–1970), a fellowship from the Council for Research on Economic History (1971–1972), and fellowships from the National Endowment for the Humanities (1973–1976). His publications include *A Short History of Western Civilization*, Eighth Edition, 1994 (co-author), *Western Civilization: Sources, Images, and Interpretations*, Fourth Edition, 1995, *World Civilizations: Sources, Images, and Interpretations*, 1994 (co-author), a series of introductions in the Garland Library of War and Peace, several articles and reviews on nineteenth-century French economic and social history in American and European journals, and short fiction in literary journals.

CONTENTS

PREFACE

This new edition of the *Study Guide* reflects changes in the Sixth Edition of *The Western Experience* and a growing interest in the connections between history and geography. Each chapter of the Sixth Edition of *The Western Experience* contains primary documents. Therefore, readings are no longer included in this edition of the *Study Guide*, but there is a new section entitled **"Guide to Documents,"** which provides questions that should indicate ways these documents can be used to increase historical understanding. The importance of maps in understanding historical developments is reflected in the expansion of the **"Map Exercises"** section of the *Study Guide*. The number of maps and accompanying exercises has been more than doubled for this new edition. Otherwise the structure of the *Study Guide* remains the same while the content has been revised to reflect the changes in the new edition of *The Western Experience*.

INTRODUCTION

WHAT IS HISTORY?

Definition

History is the record of the human past. It includes both the more concrete elements of the past such as our wars, governments, and creations, and the more elusive ones such as hopes, fantasies, and failures over time. Historians study this human past in order to discover what people thought and did, and then they organize these findings into a broad chronological framework. To do this, they look at the records humans have left of their past, the most important of which are written. Although nonwritten records, such as artifacts, buildings, oral traditions, and paintings, are also sources for the study of the human past, the period before written records appear is usually considered "pre-history."

The Purposes of History

History can be used for various purposes. First, a systematic study of the past helps us to understand human nature; in short, history can be used to give us an idea of who we are as human beings. Second, it can be used to gain insights into contemporary affairs, either through a study of the developments that have shaped the present or through the use of analogies to related circumstances of the past. Third, societies use history to socialize the young, that is, to teach them how to behave and think in culturally and socially appropriate ways.

Orientation

Historians approach the study of history from two main perspectives: the humanities and the social sciences. Those with a humanities orientation see history as being made up of unique people, actions, and events, which are to be studied both for their intrinsic value and for the insights they provide about humans in a particular set of historical circumstances. Those with a social science orientation look for patterns in human thought and behavior over time. They focus on comparisons rather than on unique events and are more willing to draw conclusions related to present problems. The authors of *The Western Experience,* Sixth Edition, use both perspectives.

Styles

In writing history, historians traditionally use two main styles: narrative and analytic. Those who prefer the narrative style emphasize a chronological sequence of events. Their histories are more like stories, describing the events from the beginning to the end. Historians who prefer the analytic style emphasize explanation. Their histories deal more with topics, focusing on causes and relationships. Most historians use both styles but show a definite preference for one or the other. The authors of *The Western Experience* stress the analytic style.

Interpretations

Some historians have a particular interpretation or philosophy of history, that is, a way of understanding its meaning and of interpreting its most important aspects. Marxist historians, for example, argue that economic forces are most important, influencing politics, culture, and society in profound ways. They view history organically, following a path in relatively predictable ways. Their interpretations are occasionally pointed out in *The Western Experience*. Most historians are not committed to a particular philosophy of history, but they do interpret major historical developments in certain ways. Thus, for example, there are various groups of historians who emphasize a social interpretation of the French Revolution of 1789, while there are others who argue that the Revolution is best understood in political and economic terms. The authors of *The Western Experience* are relatively eclectic; they use a variety of interpretations and often indicate major points of interpretive disagreement among historians.

Common Concerns

The style, orientation, and philosophy of most modern historians are not at one extreme or the other. Moreover, the concerns they share outweigh their differences. All historians want to know what happened, when it happened, and how it happened. While the question of cause is touchy, historians all want to know why something happened, and they are all particularly interested in studying change over time.

THE HISTORICAL METHOD

Process

1. *Search for Sources:*   One of the first tasks a historian faces is the search for sources. Most sources are written documents, which include everything from gravestone inscriptions and diaries to books and governmental records. Other sources include buildings, art, maps, pottery, and oral traditions. In searching for sources, historians do not work at random. They usually have something in mind before they start, and in the process, they must decide which sources to emphasize over others.

2. *External Criticism:* To test the genuineness of the source, historians must engage in external criticism. This constitutes an attempt to uncover forgeries and errors. Some startling revisions of history have resulted from effective criticism of previously accepted sources.

3. *Internal Criticism:* A source, though genuine, may not be objective, or it may reveal something that was not apparent at first. To deal with this, historians subject sources to internal criticism by such methods as evaluating the motives of the person who wrote the document, looking for inconsistencies within the source, and comparing different meanings of a word or phrase used in the source.

4. *Synthesis:* Finally, the historian creates a synthesis. He or she gathers the relevant sources together, applies them to the question being investigated, decides what is to be included, and writes a history. This oversimplifies the process, for historians often search, criticize, and synthesize at the same time. Moreover, the process is not as objective as it seems, for historians select what they think is most important and what fits into their own philosophy or interpretation of history.

Categories

Historians use certain categories to organize different types of information. The number and boundaries of these differ according to what each historian thinks is most useful. The principal categories are as follows:

1. *Political:* This refers to questions of how humans are governed, including such matters as the exercise of power in peace and war, the use of law, the formation of governments, the collection of taxes, and the establishment of public services.

2. *Economic:* This refers to the production and distribution of goods and services. On the production side, historians usually focus on agriculture, commerce, manufacturing, and finance. On the distribution side, they deal with who gets how much of what is produced. Their problem is supply and demand and how people earn their living.

3. *Social:* This is the broadest category. It refers to relations between individuals or groups within some sort of community. This includes the institutions people create (the family, the army), the classes or castes to which people belong (the working class, the aristocracy), the customs people follow (marriage, eating), the activities people engage in together (sports, drinking), and the attitudes people share (toward foreigners, commerce).

4. *Intellectual:* This refers to the ideas, theories, and beliefs expressed by people in some organized way about topics thought to be important. This includes such matters as political theories, scientific ideas, and philosophies of life.

5. *Religious:* This refers to theories, beliefs, and practices related to the supernatural or the unknown. This includes such matters as the growth of religious institutions, the formation of beliefs about the relation between human beings and God, and the practice of rituals and festivals.

6. *Cultural:* This refers to the ideas, values, and expressions of human beings as evidenced in aesthetic works, such as music, art, and literature.

In addition to organizing different types of information into categories, historians often specialize in one or two of these. For example, some historians focus on political history, whereas others are concerned with social-economic history. The best historians bring to bear on the problems that interest them, however specialized the problems may seem, data from all these categories.

DOCUMENTS

Historians classify written documents into two types: primary and secondary. Primary documents are those written by a person living during the period being studied and participating in the matter under investigation. A primary document is looked at as a piece of evidence that shows what people thought, how they acted, and what they accomplished. A secondary document is usually written by someone after the period of time that is being studied. It is either mainly a description or an interpretation of the topic being studied: the more descriptive it is, the more it simply traces what happened; the more interpretive it is, the more it analyzes the causes or the significance of what happened.

PERIODIZATION

Historians cannot deal with all of history at once. One way to solve this is to break history up into separate periods. How this is done is a matter of discretion; what is important is the division of a time into periods that can be dealt with as a whole, without doing too much violence to the continuity of history. Typically, Western Civilization is divided into the Ancient World, the Middle Ages, the Renaissance and Reformation, the Early Modern World, the nineteenth century (1789–1914), and the twentieth century (1914–present), as illustrated by the section summaries in this study guide. There are a number of subdivisions that can be made within these periods. *The Western Experience* is divided into both periodic and topical chapters.

STUDY AIDS

Reading

There is no way to get around reading—the more you read, the better you become at it. Thus the best advice is to read the assigned chapters. But there are some techniques that will make the task easier. First, think about the title of the book you are reading; often, it tells much about what is in the book. Second, read through the chapter headings and subheadings. Whatever you read will make more sense and will be more easily remembered if it is placed in the context of the section, the chapter, and the book as a whole. Third, concentrate on the first and last paragraphs or two of each chapter and each major section of the chapter. Often, the author will summarize in these areas what he or she wants to communicate. Finally, concentrate on the first sentence of each paragraph. Often, but not always, the first sentence is a topic sentence, making the point for which the rest of the paragraph is an expansion.

Note Taking

1. *Reading Assignments:* While it is easier said than done, it is of tremendous advantage to take notes on reading assignments. Taking notes, if done properly, will help you to integrate the readings into your mind much more than simply reading them. Moreover, notes will ease the problem of review for papers, exams, or classroom discussions.

There are a number of ways to take notes. Generally, you should use an outline form, following the main points or headings of each chapter. Under each section of your outline you should include the important points and information, translated into your own words. After each section of a chapter ask yourself, "What is the author trying to say here, what is the author trying to convey?" It may be easier to copy phrases or words used by the author, but it is much more effective if you can transform them into your own words. While facts, names, and dates are important, avoid simply making a list of them without focusing on the more general interpretation, development, or topic that the author is discussing. Indicate the kinds of evidence the author uses, what the author's interpretations are, and to what degree you agree with what he or she says (does it make sense to you?). Some students prefer to underline in the text and write notes in the margins. This is a less time-consuming, easier, and often useful method, but probably not as effective as outlining and using your own words to summarize each section. As with many things, it is the extra effort involved that leads to the more effective learning.

2. *Lectures and Classes:* Much of what has been said also applies to taking notes in class, except that it is more difficult. The trick is to write just enough to get the main points without losing track of what is going on in class. A couple of techniques might help. It is crucial to be ready at the beginning of class. Often, the point of a whole lecture or discussion is outlined in the first couple of minutes; missing it makes much of what you hear seem out of context.

Take notes. Putting this off often leads to a passive state of listening, and soon, daydreaming, at which point much of what is said will go in one ear and out the other. Concentrate on the major points the speaker is trying to make, not simply all the facts. Do not try to write down everything or to write in complete sentences; try to develop a method of writing down key words or phrases that works for you. Finally, try to go over your notes after class.

Writing

There are three steps that should be taken before you actually start writing a paper. First, carefully read the question or topic you are to write on; at times, good papers are written on the wrong topic. If you are to make up a topic, spend some time on it. Think of your topic as a question. It should not be unanswerably broad (what is the history of Western Civilization?) or insignificantly narrow (when was toothpaste invented?). It will be something that interests you and that is easily researched. Second, start reading about the topic, taking notes on the main points. Third, after some reading, start writing an outline of the main points you want to make. Revise this outline a number of times, arranging your points in some logical way and making sure all your points help answer the question or support the argument you are making.

A paper should have three parts: an introduction, a body, and a conclusion. For a short paper, you introduction should be only a paragraph or two in length; for a long paper, perhaps one or two pages. In the introduction tell the reader what the general topic is, what you will argue about the topic, and why it is important or interesting. This is an extremely important part of a paper, often neglected by students. You can win or lose the reader with the introduction. You may find it easier to leave the introduction until after you have written the body of the paper, especially if it is difficult to get started writing. In the body, make your argument. Generally, make one major point in each paragraph, usually in the first sentence (topic sentence). The rest of the paragraph should contain explanation, expansion, support, illustration, or evidence for this point. In the paragraph, you should make it clear how this point helps answer the question. Your paragraphs should be organized in some logical order (chronological, from strongest to weakest point, categories). Finally, in the conclusion, tell the reader—in different words—what you have argued in the body of the paper, and indicate why what you have argued is important. The conclusion, like the introduction, is a particularly important and yet an often slighted part of a paper.

Most of the same suggestions for papers apply to essay exams. Even more emphasis should be placed on making sure you know what the question asks. Spend some time outlining your answer. As with papers, you should have an introduction, body, and conclusion, even if they are all relatively short. For each point you make, try to supply some evidence as support. Keep to the indicated time limits.

Class Participation

Class participation is difficult for many students, yet there is no better way to get over this difficulty than to do it. Try and force yourself to ask questions or indicate your point of view when appropriate times arise. If this is particularly difficult for you, it may help to talk about it with other students or with the teacher privately.

Studying

If you have a style of studying that works well for you, stick to it. If not, try to do three things: keep up with all your assignments regularly, work with someone else, and spend some extra time reviewing before exams.

HOW TO USE THIS GUIDE

There is one chapter in this guide corresponding to each chapter in *The Western Experience*. Each chapter of the guide is divided into a number of sections.

1. *Main Themes:* The main themes of each chapter are introduced here. Part of the purpose in doing this is to emphasize the importance of not losing sight of the broader concerns of the chapter as you study its specific sections. By returning to these main themes and expanding upon them after you read the chapter, they can become a tool to help you grasp more firmly what the chapter is about.

2. *Outline and Summary:* Here, the chapter in the text is outlined and summarized. The outline headings are the same as those in the text. Under each heading, the main points, with supporting information, are indicated. Keep in mind that everything cannot be included in this summary. It is designed as a guide, summary, and supplement to the text.

3. *Guide to Documents:* Each chapter contains questions related to the documents used in *The Western Experience*. The questions are designed to show how those documents might be used to increase historical understanding and gain insights into historical questions.

4. *Significant Individuals:* Here, the principal historical figures mentioned in the text are listed with some brief biographical information. This is intended to be used in two ways: first, as a reference; and second, as an exercise. You should be able to state, briefly, who each person is and why that person is important. Emphasis should be placed on the significance of the person's thoughts or actions.

5. *Chronological Diagram:* This diagram is intended to be used as a reference. Note what different sorts of events are related chronologically. It is often useful to compare the chronological chart in one chapter with those in the preceding and succeeding chapters. On an even broader scale, this is done in the chronological diagrams contained in each section summary.

6. *Map Exercises:* In most chapters maps are provided with exercises that relate to some of the main concerns of the chapter. Standing alone and without directly using the text, some of these exercises are difficult. But by utilizing the maps already present in the text and in some cases specific sections of the text referred to in the exercise, they become easier. The purposes here are to help you get used to using maps, to emphasize the importance of geographic considerations in history, and to encourage you to picture developments described in the text in concrete, geographic terms.

7. *Identification:* Some of the most important developments or events in the chapter are listed here. For each, you should indicate what the development or event was, when it occurred, and what its significance was (why was it important?).

8. *Problems for Analysis:* These are designed to cover each of the main sections of the chapter. They require a combination of specific information and analysis. Working on these problems should give you a much stronger grasp of the materials and issues dealt with in each section of the chapter. In addition, you might use some of these problems to prepare for class discussions. They might help you formulate questions to ask in class or present a point of view that you find particularly interesting or irritating.

9. *Speculations:* These constitute unusual, interesting questions. They may require you to put yourself back into history, compare the past with the present, or speculate on various historical alternatives. They might be used as a first step toward identifying a paper topic or developing a classroom debate. From aspects of broader speculations, more specific historical problems could be identified, put into perspective, and dealt with.

10. *Transitions:* These relate the previous chapter, the present chapter, and the following chapter. One of the main purposes here is to help you avoid losing the continuity of history; each chapter in the text is integrally connected to what came before and what follows. Another purpose is to emphasize briefly the main arguments presented in the chapter; focusing on specific events can sometimes lead one to overlook the broader conclusions that are being drawn.

In addition to the chapters, there are six section summaries; these correspond to periods into which historians commonly divide Western history and to sections of the book often covered in an exam or a paper. Each contains Chronological Diagrams, Map Exercises, and Box Charts for you to fill in. Tabulating material from your reading notes on these charts (which you will need to reproduce in larger format in your notebook or on separate sheets of paper) will help you place individuals and events in a broader chronological framework, identify historical turning points, better understand developments that span long periods of time and several chapters, and distinguish important facts from less important ones. The charts should be particularly useful when you are reviewing for an exam.

Dennis Sherman

A STUDY GUIDE AND MAP SUPPLEMENT FOR

THE
WESTERN
EXPERIENCE

VOLUME I
TO THE EIGHTEENTH CENTURY

ONE
THE FIRST
CIVILIZATIONS

MAIN THEMES

1. Humans became food producers rather than food gatherers some 12,000 years ago with the development of agriculture, the essential step in the creation of complex civilizations.
2. As cities were established in the river valleys of Mesopotamia, the early Sumerian and Babylonian civilizations emerged.
3. Egyptians developed a prosperous, long-lasting, religious society along the Nile between about 3000 and 300 B.C.E.
4. After 1650 the Hittites established a powerful state in the Near East, but between 1250 and 1100, invaders utilizing iron weapons ended the Hittite domination and brought the Bronze Age to an end.
5. In Palestine, the Phoenicians created a sophisticated urban civilization, and the Israelites developed a short-lived kingdom but an enduring religious and cultural tradition.
6. The Assyrians—followed by the Chaldeans, the Medes, and the Persians—established powerful unifying empires in the Near East.

OUTLINE AND SUMMARY

Human beings first settled in agricultural villages around 8000 B.C.E. After about 3000, early civilizations and then powerful kingdoms arose along river valleys in Asia Minor and Egypt.

I. The Earliest Humans

Homo sapiens have inhabited the earth for the last 350,000 years. Scholars think that the immediate predecessor, Homo erectus, emerged about 1,500,000 years ago. Humanity probably originated in east Africa some 2 million years ago.

1. Human Beings as Food Gatherers

For most of their existence, human beings got food by hunting and gathering. During this long period, known as the Old Stone Age or Paleolithic Age, men

1

and women probably shared many tasks, but women may have specialized in tending the crops and bearing the young. Men may have specialized in hunting and defense, perhaps thereby becoming politically and socially dominant. Cave paintings reveal connections between symbolic action, art, thought, and religion.

2. Human Beings as Food Producers

About 10,000 B.C.E. the Neolithic Revolution—the rise of agriculture—occurred. Perhaps caused by climatic changes and increasing population resulting in a need for new food supplies, this revolution led to long-term planning, specialization, new technologies, trade, and territorial wars.

3. Early Near Eastern Villages

Between 9000 and 6000 B.C.E. villages arose in the hills of the Near East. Over time, communal gods, domesticated animals, new technologies, trade, and new regulation of social behavior arose in these communities.
IN what is Now Southern Turkey and NoRTER Iraq

II. The First Civilizations in Mesopotamia

1. The Emergence of Civilization

Civilization, first arising about 3000 B.C.E., was marked by a complex social organization as well as the establishment of political authority, the creation of laws and legal codes, the growth of cities with occupational specialization (often thanks to slavery), the establishment of priests, and the development of new arts and crafts.

2. Sumer

The first cities appeared in Sumer in southern Mesopotamia. By the beginning of the Bronze Age (about 3000 B.C.E.), there were a number of independent city-states in the area. Citizens were divided into three classes (nobles and priests, commoners, and slaves) ruled by a king who depended upon support from the priests and nobles. The cities were marked by tall temples (ziggurats) single-story houses, and active trade. Sumerians created a system of mathematical notation, an efficient form of writing ("cuneiform"), and literary religious myths (*The Creation of Mankind*). The Sumerian cities were weakened by continual warfare, and in 2371 they fell to the invading Semitic-speaking Akkadians under the warlord Sargon. The Sumerians regained control after the dissolution of the Akkadian kingdom about 2230. The first law codes date from this Third Dynasty of Ur.

3. The Babylonian Kingdom

In about 2000 B.C.E. a Semitic people, the Amorites, succeeded the Sumerians, eventually forming the powerful kingdom of Babylonia under Hammurabi

(1792–1750 B.C.E.). The Code of Hammurabi reveals much about Babylonian laws and politics as well as about social and sexual divisions within Babylonian society.

4. Mesopotamian Culture

Mesopotamians developed relatively complex mathematics, astrology, and astronomy.

III. Egypt

Egypt, arising around and dependent upon the Nile River, achieved great permanence.

1. The Old Kingdom

Around 3000 B.C.E., Menes unified Egypt. During the Old Kingdom (2700–2200) the king acquired absolute power as owner of the land and as a living god. Between 2600 and 2500 the great pyramids at Giza were constructed.

   a.   *Religion:*   The king and a number of associated and lesser gods presided over Egyptian civilization. Egyptians believed in a relatively pleasant life after death and devoted much effort in preparation for it. The arts of embalming and pyramid building testify to this.

   b.   *Maat:*   Egyptians thought abstractly about ethical qualities, as indicated by their belief in *maat* ("right order").

   c.   *Writing:*   The Egyptians developed their pictorial and phonetic form of writing (hieroglyphics) and writing material (papyri).

   d.   *Literature:*   Egyptians produced a variety of religious myths (the *Book of the Dead*), "instructions" on how to get ahead in the world, love poems, and fables.

   e.   *Mathematics and Medicine:*   Egyptians mastered surveying and applied mathematics to deal with the changing Nile. In medicine, they went beyond magic by using an empirical approach to illness.

   f.   *The Invasion of the Hyksos:*   Around 1720 the Hyksos invaded and controlled parts of Egypt until 1570, when Egyptian warriors drove them out and initiated the New Kingdom.

2. The New Kingdom

Pharaohs from Thebes strengthened the central government, created a military state, and expanded the kingdom into Asia Minor.

   a.   *Hatshepsut:*   Rulers such at Hatshepsut and Thutmose III built up and expanded the state. Conquest brought tribute, slaves, trade, and prosperity.

   b.   *Akhnaton's Religious Reform:*   King Amenhotep IV (Akhnaton) attempted a major religious reform, which was connected with efforts to overcome the power of priests and bureaucrats, by sponsoring the worship of Aton over the traditional god Amen-Re. Religiously, Akhnaton was, at best, tempo-rarily successful; but politically, his authority disintegrated. He was succeeded by more traditional pharaohs such as Ramses II, who reestablished Amen-Re, gained political dominance within Egypt, and continued the construction of massive monuments.

3. A View of Egyptian Society

From slaves and peasants at the bottom to priests and kings at the top, Egyptian society survived for some 3000 years. Some social mobility was possible, and Egyptian society was relatively liberal in the scope given to women.

IV. The Early Indo-Europeans

After about 6000 to 5000 B.C.E. Indo-Europeans—groups of linguistically related peoples who had congregated within one area of Europe near the Caucasus mountains in Southern Russia, began spreading across Europe and parts of Asia.

1. The Hittite Kingdom

By 1650, the Hittites, an Indo-European people, established a capital at Hattusha (in modern Turkey). Over the next 400 years, they expanded to become the most formidable state in Asia Minor. Their king, though dependent on elite families, served as general, chief judge, and high priest. Their society was patriarchal, though women did have some rights.

2. The Close of the Bronze Age

The period between about 1250 and 1150 was one of upheaval in Asia Minor, probably brought on by the iron age. The use by invaders of iron for weapons broke up the Hittite kingdom. Moreover, the use of iron, which was cheaper and more available than bronze, meant that more people could acquire the power that weapons brought.

V. Palestine

1. Canaanites and Phoenicians

By 1200 Canaanites had established themselves in Phoenicia and went on to create a sophisticated urban civilization. Their influence was spread by their navies, their trading posts, and their development of a simplified alphabet.

2. Hebrew Society

The Old Testament can serve as a useful, historical document. In forming their history of the Israelites, the writers of the Old Testament used traditional materials and emphasized one god and his relationship to humans.

a. *The Early Hebrews:* Between about 1900 and 1200, Israelite tribes migrated into various parts of the Near East and Egypt. Around 1270 Moses unified many of these tribes with some Canaanites under a god conventionally called Yahweh, and a complex code of ethically based laws. Women were severely restricted in early Israelite society.

b. *The Israelite Monarchy:* The Israelite tribes successfully invaded Canaanite territory and eventually unified and formed a central government under a line of strong kings (Saul, David, and Solomon) between 1020 and 920. After the autocratic and extravagant Solomon, the kingdom split into two parts: the northern, eventually conquered by Assyria in 722, and the southern, finally falling in 586 to the Chaldeans. The Israelites were dispersed, though there were occasional revivals of an independent Jewish kingdom in Palestine.

c. *The Faith and the Prophets:* Over time, Judaism was shaped by a series of social critics (prophets)—who emphasized corruption, moral reform, and a redeeming Messiah—and a series of scholars—who organized the sacred writings of Judaism. 445 BC, EZRA published the First FIVE Books of the OLD TESTAMENT /

3. The Jewish Legacy

The Jews have persisted as a society over the centuries, and their monotheistic religion became extraordinarily influential.

VI. The Near Eastern Empires

The Assyrians were the first to unify politically the Near East. They were followed by the Persians.

1. The Assyrian State

The militaristic Assyrians conquered most of the Near East between about 900 and 700. They ruled their vast empire both directly and indirectly, extracting tribute everywhere. The Semitic language known as Aramaic was spoken throughout the area. Their cultural legacy remains in their art (reliefs at Niveveh) and cuneiform texts.

2. The Chaldeans and the Medes

The Assyrians fell to the Chaldeans, based in Babylon, and the Medes, located further east. The Chaldeans are best known for their superb astronomers and for their capital city, with its lavish temples built by Nebuchadnezzar. The Medes established their kingdom around 625, but it soon fell to the Persians.

3. The Persian Empire

King Cyrus (559–530) formed the Persian Empire by conquering the Medes to the north, the Lydians to the west, and the Chaldeans to the south. His successor, Cambyses, conquered Egypt in 525. Darius (521–486) divided the empire effectively into some 20 provinces ruled by satraps and linked it together with a system of roads. The king was not divine. During the 500s the Persian priest and reformer Zoroaster (Zarathustra) formed the Persian faith. Zoroaster taught a dualistic religion, which held that there was a supreme god of truth opposed by an evil spirit. This would prove to be a popular, long-lasting, and influential religion.

GUIDE TO DOCUMENTS

Hammurabi's Law Code

1. What principles of justice are reflected in these laws?
2. What do these laws reveal about the rights of women in Babylonia?

The Salvation of Israel

1. What does this reveal about the Israelite perception of God and God's relationship to the Israelites?
2. How does this document explain the escape of the Israelites from Egypt? How might this explanation be evaluated?

Jeremiah Reproaches Israel

1. Compare this document with the previous document on the salvation of Israel. How does this document add to our understanding of the Israelite perception of God?
2. What does this reveal about the sorts of problems experienced by the people of Israel?

SIGNIFICANT INDIVIDUALS

Kings

Sargon (2371–2316), Akkad.
Ur-Nammu (2113–2096), Ur.
Hammurabi (1792–1750), Babylonia.
Suppiluliumas (ca. 1380–1340), Hittite.
Amenhotep IV (1369?–1353?), Egypt
Ramses II (1292–1225), Egypt.

Saul (ca. 1020), Israel.
David (1010?–960?), Israel.
Solomon (960?–920?), Israel.
Ashurbanipal (668–627?), Assyria.
Nebuchadnezzar (604–562), Chaldea.
Cyrus (559–530), Persia.
Croesus (580?–546), Lydia.
Darius (521–486), Persia.

Religious Leaders

Moses (ca. 1270), Israelite prophet.

Zoroaster (Zarathustra) (ca. 600), Persian priest and reformer.

CHRONOLOGICAL DIAGRAM

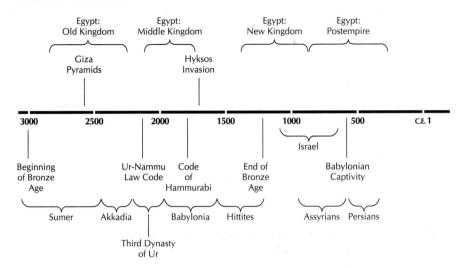

IDENTIFICATION

Homo sapiens

Bronze Age

Code of Hammurabi

maat

hieroglyphics

ziggurat

cuneiform

Amen-Re

Aton

Indo-European

Zoroastrianism

MAP EXERCISES

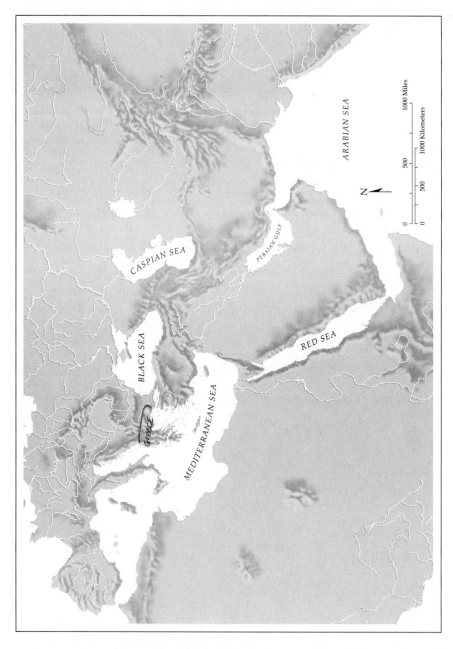

1. Locate areas where early civilizations arose.
2. Show the direction where major invaders came from.
3. Show areas of likely interaction between civilizations.

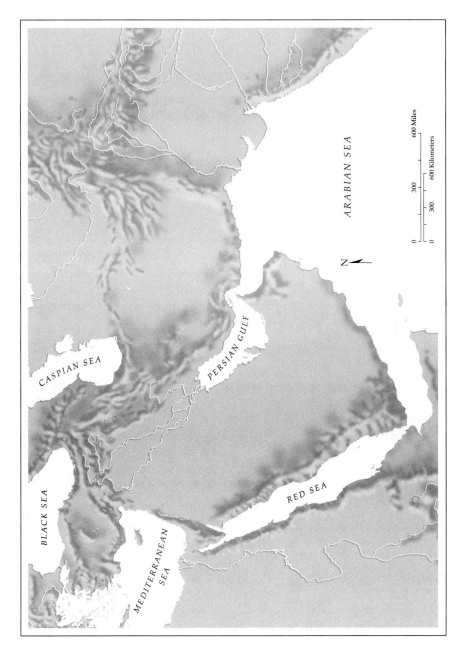

1. Indicate the approximate boundaries of Egypt, the Assyrian Empire, the Hittite kingdom, the Hebrew kingdom, and the Persian Empire at their heights.
2. Indicate the main river valleys in the area.
3. Indicate the location of some early agricultural sites.

PROBLEMS FOR ANALYSIS

I. *The Earliest Humans*

1. Why was the development of agriculture so crucial for the establishment of civilization? What advantages do food producers have over food gatherers?

II. *The First Civilizations in Mesopotamia*

1. In what ways was the rise of Sumerian cities a significant development in Western history? Describe the characteristics of Sumerian civilization.
2. How has analysis of cuneiform inscriptions and codes revealed much about Babylonian politics, society, and culture?

III. *Egypt*

1. Compare Egyptian civilization with Mesopotamia. What role did the Nile play in the development of Egyptian civilization?
2. What do Egyptian attitudes toward life after death reveal about the Egyptian religion and attitudes toward life in general?

IV. *The Early Indo-Europeans*

1. In what ways were the Hittites unique, and in what ways did they adapt to conditions in areas they conquered?
2. Why was the introduction of iron so important?

V. *Palestine*

1. What explains the extraordinary influence of the Canaanites and Phoenicians?
2. How useful is the Old Testament as a historical document? Explain.
3. How did the religion of the Israelites become so influential in Western civilization?

VI. *The Near Eastern Empires*

1. Using examples from the Assyrians and Persians, explain how Near Eastern kings were able to hold their vast empires together.

SPECULATIONS

1. Explain what you think prompted people to initiate the first civilizations. How do you explain the development of civilizations in different places during the same period of time?

2. What are the advantages and disadvantages of civilization? Use examples from Egyptian or Near Eastern civilizations.
3. Given the historical conditions of the time, if you were a Persian king in the year 550, how would you organize your empire? Why?

TRANSITIONS

In "The First Civilizations," the nature and beginnings of Western civilization in the Near East and Egypt are examined. The development of agriculture in these river valleys was the crucial step allowing greater numbers of people to support themselves, enabling the production of surplus food, facilitating specialization, and stimulating the growth of more complex societies. These changes were furthered through the growth of cities and imperial expansion, consolidating the transition to civilized conditions. Early civilizations discovered different ways to deal with the problems of how people relate to each other and to divine forces. Some of the peoples in this area—such as the Egyptians, Assyrians, and Persians—developed large and long-lasting societies; while others, such as the Israelites, left a more influential religious and ethical heritage.

In "The Forming of Greek Civilization," the focus will shift north to Greece, where a highly urbanized and extraordinarily sophisticated civilization developed.

TWO
THE FORMING OF
GREEK CIVILIZATION

MAIN THEMES

1. Early Greek civilization was dominated by Crete (the Minoan civilization) and independent city-states (most prominently, Mycenae). This age was brought to a close by the Dorian invasions around 1100, which ushered in a Dark Age of some 300 years.
2. Greek civilization revived after 800, as indicated by the flowering of Homeric epic poetry, the establishment of numerous Greek colonies, the development of an unusual set of religious beliefs, and the creation of uniquely Hellenic literature and art.
3. Greek political, social, and economic life was centered around the *polis,* whose organization and government evolved into different forms over time, as exemplified by the contrasting Spartan and Athenian experiences.
4. The Greeks unified themselves and gained stunning victories over the invading Persians, thereby preserving their independence.
5. After the Persian Wars, Athens rose to dominance in the Greek world, attaining its height during the Age of Pericles.
6. The Peloponnesian War proved disastrous for Athens and many other Greek city-states.

OUTLINE AND SUMMARY

The Greeks developed an extraordinarily creative civilization. The civic culture of their city-states was a marked departure from traditional Near Eastern monarchy. Athens and Sparta became leading, contrasting rivals.

I. Crete and Early Greece (Ca. 3000–1100 B.C.E.)

The history of Greece begins with the people of the island of Crete.

1. Cretan Civilization

Much of our information about Cretan civilization comes from evidence found in the Palace of Minos at Knossos, built between 2200 and 1500. Minoan art was colorful, and the absence of defensive walls suggests that

Minoan civilization was peaceful. Women occupied an important place in this society. The wealth of Crete came from trade.

2. Crete and the Greeks

Minoan civilization reached its height between 1500 and 1400 and strongly influenced the Greeks. Their Linear A and Linear B writing tablets have survived, and the latter have been deciphered and evidence a Greek influence or dominance toward the civilization's end. About 1380 some sort of violent disaster, perhaps the combined effects of earthquakes and rebellions, engulfed Cretan cities.

3. Mycenaean Civilization (Ca. 1600–1100 B.C.E.)

Arriving from the north, the Greeks (Hellenes) began to settle in Greece about 2000. The mountainous geography helped split the Greeks into independent political communities. By 1600 Greeks had established a number of prosperous city-states; until its fall around 1100, Mycenae was the most prominent. As revealed by excavated graves and monuments and by Linear B tablets, Mycenae was a rich kingdom. The other city-states were probably independent under their own kings, though they once seem to have formed a league against Troy, a prosperous city in Asia Minor. Excavations of Troy support at least parts of Homer's accounts of the Greek expedition against Troy. The Mycenaean Age was brought to a close around 1100 by invaders, perhaps Dorians, ending forever the domination of palace-centered kings. From 1100 to 800, Greece entered a Dark Age, her culture disintegrating to the point of a loss of writing skills.

II. The Greek Renaissance (Ca. 800–600 B.C.E.)

Greek culture and civilization revived after the Dark Age.

1. Greek Religion

Greek gods were anthropomorphic beings with distinct personalities who intervened actively in human affairs. Greek religion did not include a rigorous religious code of behavior or a separate priestly class. Religion served to support the life of individual cities. It also supported a common Panhellenic culture throughout Greece (Olympia, Delphi).

2. Public Games

Panhellenic games, initiated in 776, brought together Greek culture and religion while celebrating human perfection and heroism.

3. Colonization (Ca. 750–550 B.C.E.)

Between 750 and 550 Greeks, perhaps because of a growing population and limited resources, established colonies throughout the Mediterranean. This resulted in growing trade and prosperity and the spread of Greek civilization.

4. *The Alphabet*

Greeks adapted the Phoenician alphabet, creating two versions of their own that would spread throughout the Western world and that would stimulate Greek civilization. GREEK ALPHABET ABOUT 750 BC

5. *Archaic Literature*

The Homeric epics, the *Iliad* and the *Odyssey,* were the greatest of the epic poems that appeared after 750. The themes of the *Iliad* include the heroism of the warrior aristocracy and men and women in conflict. The *Odyssey* explores human character and behavior. The author is unknown; probably the poems were composed orally and later written down. Greek poets adapted the legacy of the Homeric epics to create a more personal literature, as with Hesiod's *Work and Days* and the lyric poetry of Archilochus and Sappho.

III. *The Polis*

1. *Organization and Government*

The independent city-state, the polis, consisted of a city built around a citadel (acropolis), the surrounding area of farms, and its community of citizens. In the early poleis local kings were powerful, but by 700 they had generally been replaced by landowning oligarchies who governed through small counsils on assemblies. In the seventh and sixth centuries, political power spread toward ordinary citizens, as indicated by new legal codes. At this time, also, popular leaders ("tyrants") emerged to challenge the rule of the wealthier classes.
GREEKS LACKED (by choice) A PRIESTLY CLASS

2. *The Economy of the Poleis (Ca. 700–400* B.C.E.*)*

Economic life centered predominantly around agriculture, but homeland Greeks often relied on trade and colonization to feed themselves. Most Greeks lived modestly. After 625 the use of coins developed, but only slowly. Most major public expenses were assigned to the rich.

   a. *The Roles of the Sexes:* Men were the rulers and leaders. The roles women could play were restricted by men. Evidence indicated that the Greeks held conflicting attitudes toward women. Women were controled Bearing children made men fear them

   b. *Slavery:* Slavery was accepted in Greece as well as in all ancient societies. Manual labor was looked down upon by Greeks; slaves were relied on, particularly for craft, domestic, and industrial labor.

3. *Sparta and Athens (Ca. 700–500* B.C.E.*)*

Though atypical, we know most about Sparta and Athens.

   a. *Sparta:* Sparta, the leader of the Dorian states in the Peloponnesus, became a militaristic state in the eighth century, in response to population problems and in order to control the numerous Messenian (helot) subjects. Reforms in the seventh century created a mixed oligarchic constitution.

Sometime after 530 the Spartans formed the Peloponnesian League, seeking strength through alliance rather than conquest. Sparta rigorously trained its children, avoided foreign contacts, and did not encourage development of the arts. *A woman could bear children out of wed Lock for the good of SPARTA*

b. *Athens:* Athens, an unusually large and commercial polis, experimented politically more than any other city-state. Before 683, Athens was ruled by a king. Thereafter it was ruled by an assembly, elected administrators (archons), and a council (the Areopagus). Around 621 Draco instituted legal reforms. Reacting to growing economic and social problems, Solon instituted a series of reforms, probably in the 570s, that freed peasants from agricultural debts, prevented civil war, encouraged commerce, and ended privileges based on birth (but not property). In the middle of the sixth century Pisistratus seized power, weakened the power of the aristocracy, encouraged industry and trade, and initiated a program of public works. Around 508 Cleisthenes instituted far-reaching reforms, reorganizing Athens socially and politically. Over time, more male citizens became directly involved in government and the judicial system, often holding important offices through rotation of service or election by lot. *for councillors was called Demokratia*

IV. The Challenge of Persia

At the beginning of the "classical" period of Greek history the Greeks faced a great challenge from Persia.

1. The Invasion under Darius and Marathon (490 B.C.E.)

Angered by Athenian support of the Ionian Revolt (499), Darius of Persia attacked the Athenians at Marathon and Athens in 490. He suffered stinging losses.

2. The Second Persian War (480–479 B.C.E.)

Darius' son Xerxes prepared for a much greater attack. Meanwhile Athens, at the urging of Themistocles, built up its navy and allied itself with some 30 city-states under Spartan leadership. The first battle was at Thermopylae in 480, a costly Persian victory. The Persians burned an abandoned Athens but succumbed to the strategy of Themistocles, who led the Greeks to a stunning naval victory at Salamis. In 479 the Greeks decisively defeated the Persian army at Plataea and then at Mycale in Asia Minor.

V. The Wars of the Fifth Century (479–404 B.C.E.)

1. The Athenian Empire

In 478–477, after Sparta's return to isolationism, a number of city-states, under the leadership of Athens, formed a confederation—the Delian League—for protection and continued war against Persia. By the 450s the league had succeeded against Persia and evolved into the Athenian Empire, with Athens benefiting from contributions to the treasury.

2. The Age of Pericles

Athens reached its height during the Age of Pericles (459–429). Pericles, an aristocratic leader who functioned as champion of the masses, rebuilt the Acropolis, strengthened the Athenian Empire, and encouraged further democratization of the Athenian judicial system.

3. The Peloponnesian War (431–404 B.C.E.)

In the 430s provocative actions by the Athenians led the Peloponnesian League, headed by Sparta, to declare a preventive war on Athens. Lasting for almost 30 years, the Peloponnesian War pitted the dominant Greek naval power, the Athenian Empire, against the dominant Greek land power, the Peloponnesian League. Years of indecisive but costly struggle and missed opportunities for peace were ended in 413, when Athens lost a crucial naval and land battle in an ambitious expedition against Syracuse, in Sicily. Athens fought on for nine more years until it was decisively beaten by Sparta. Athens lost its empire, most of its navy, and much of its trade. Political leadership and vitality were diminished. Athenian intellectuals became pessimistic, particularly about democracy, as is revealed in their political philosophy. In general, the Greek poleis were weakened by a long-lasting loss of manpower and leadership.

GUIDE TO DOCUMENTS

The Debate over Black Athena

1. Bernal and Lefkowitz offer opposing views. In these excerpts, which is the most convincing? Why?
2. Many people consider this scholarly debate extraordinarily important. Why do you think this is so?

Sappho's Love Poetry

1. What might this reveal about the existence of romantic love in Greek civilization?
2. Does this provide good evidence for the position of women in Greek civilization?

"They Have a Master Called Law"

1. What, according to this work by Herodotus, was the Greek view of the difference between rule by a man and rule by law?
2. What seems to be the message of the Spartan Demaratus? Should what he says about the Spartans be considered valid for all Greeks?

SIGNIFICANT INDIVIDUALS

Political Leaders

Lycurgus, a legendary Spartan
 lawgiver.
Draco (ca. 621), Athenian
 lawgiver.
Solon (ca. 630–ca. 559), Athenian
 lawgiver.
Pisistratus (590?–527), Athenian
 tyrant.

Cleisthenes (ca. 508), Athenian
 lawgiver.
Darius (521–486), king of Persia.
Xerxes (486–465), king of Persia.
Pericles (490?–429), Athenian
 statesman.
Alcibiades (450?–404), Athenian
 statesman.

Poets

Homer (8th century?), epic poet.
Hesiod (ca. 700), epic poet.
Sappho of Lesbos (ca. 600), lyric poet.

Archilochus of Paros (ca. 650), lyric
 poet.

IDENTIFICATION

Palace of Minos
Linear B
Trojan War
Dorian invasions
the *Iliad*
Panhellenic games
polis
"tyrants"

helots
archons
Cleisthenes' *demokratia*
Council of 500
Ionian revolt
Salamis
Delian League
Peloponnesian League

CHRONOLOGICAL DIAGRAMS

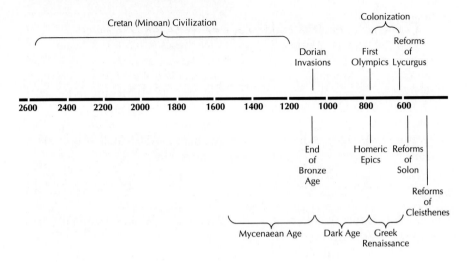

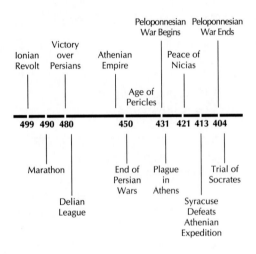

MAP EXERCISES

1. Indicate the approximate location of Mycenae, Crete, Troy, Sparta, Athens, Ionia, Miletus, Peloponnese, Attica, and the Aegean Sea.
2. Compare this map with those in Chapter 1. Describe the geographic differences, and indicate how these might relate to differences between the societies of the Near East and those of Greece.

1. Indicate (by shading) the principal Athenian and Spartan allies during the Peloponnesian War.

PROBLEMS FOR ANALYSIS

I. Crete and Early Greece

1. Compare the Cretan and Mycenaean civilizations. What evidence is there for contact between these two civilizations?
2. In what ways did Greece enter a Dark Age between 1100 and 800? Was this an unmitigated disaster? Why?

II. The Greek Renaissance

1. Analyze the religious and cultural importance of the Homeric epics.
2. In what ways did colonization lead to significant changes in Greek economic, social, and political life?
3. Analyze some of the main themes of Archaic literature.

III. The Polis

1. How was the polis organized?
2. Analyze the position of women in Greek society.
3. Compare Sparta and Athens. What were the advantages and disadvantages of the various political and social choices these two city-states made?
4. Trace the development of more democratic institutions in Athens. What were the main problems in shaping this development?

IV. The Challenge of Persia

1. How do you explain the Greek victory over the Persians, despite the overwhelming odds?

V. The Wars of the Fifth Century

1. How was Athens able to rise to such a position of leadership in the Greek world? How did its role in the Persian War contribute to this? How important was Pericles?
2. Considering that Athens survived and remained independent, what was so particularly disastrous about the Peloponnesian War?

SPECULATIONS

1. How do you explain the development of such an extraordinary civilization by the Greeks? Do you think much of the credit belongs to some sort of Greek "spirit," or were geographic factors more important?
2. Should Greek civilization be considered superior to Near Eastern civilizations, or simply different? How do you evaluate this?

TRANSITIONS

In "The First Civilizations," the origins of Western civilizations in the Near East and Egypt were examined.

In "The Forming of Greek Civilization," focus is shifted to the Aegean area. The Greeks viewed the world and human affairs in extraordinarily natural, rational, and secular terms. Greek philosophy helped create a common cultural tradition for the Western experience. Living in independent city-states, Greeks experienced changing political forms, democracy eventually spreading to an unprecedented degree. The evolution of Greek civilization, from the Minoans and Mycenaeans to the Spartans and Athenians, is traced, with emphasis on the later political developments in Athens and cultural accomplishments.

In "Classical and Hellenistic Greece," developments in Greece and the Near East during the fifth, fourth, and third centuries will be examined.

THREE
CLASSICAL AND
HELLENISTIC GREECE

MAIN THEMES

1. Athens produced extraordinarily creative dramatists, historians, architects, sculptors, and philosophers during the Classical Age (500–323).
2. Philip II and Alexander took advantage of the disunity among the Greek city-states and brought Macedonia to dominance in Greece. Alexander led a force that conquered the Persian Empire.
3. The period between the death of Alexander and that of Cleopatra is called the Hellenistic Age, a period of large warring kingdoms, great cities, relative prosperity, and important cultural accomplishments.

OUTLINE AND SUMMARY

During the fifth and fourth century the Greeks accomplished much intellectually and artistically but left themselves open to conquest by Macedonia.

I. Classical Greek Culture (Ca. 500–323 B.C.E.)

Culturally, this was an era of Athenian preeminence.

1. Greek Tragedy

Drawing on familiar tales and characters in mythology, Greek dramatists embodied religion and culture in their works. The finest dramatists dealt with such themes as the nature of justice (Aeschylus, the *Oresteia*), the tragedy of a strong leader caught in the grip of fate (Sophocles, *Oedipus the King*), and how the inner workings of a person's mind and emotions shape individual destiny (Euripides, *Medea*).

2. Comedy

Aristophanes (*Knights*) satirized political and social life in his comedies, providing us with insights into everyday life in Classical Athens.

3. Historical Writing

The Greeks produced the first serious analytic historian in the person of Herodotus. He compared Greek and Persian cultures to explain the Persian

HERODOTUS is called "father of History" he was the first to write a sustained Narrative

Wars. Thucydides (*History of the Peloponnesian War*) became the standard among ancient historians, analyzing the Peloponnesian War as a coldly realistic pursuit of power and depicting the decline of Athens after Pericles' death.

4. Philosophy

The Greeks developed philosophy—the attempt to use reason to discover why things are as they are.

a. *The Beginnings of Philosophy:* The first Greek philosophers were citizens of Miletus, wealthy commercial city whose location in Ionia enabled it to have direct contact with the ideas and achievements of the Near East. Milesians such as Thales and Anaximander developed answers to the question "What exists?' by pointing to common primal elements. Others, such as Pythagoras of Samos, turned to the study of numbers to answer this question.

b. *The Sophists and Socrates:* During the fifth century Sophists emphasized the study of human beings and how intellectual activity could be turned to practical advantage. Their ideas were an attack on accepted beliefs. Socrates (469–399) combined a reasoned pursuit of the truth through relentless questioning (the Socratic method) with ethics, thereby making him a critic of the Sophists. *Sophists turned from structure of universe to human beings/*

c. *Plato:* Socrates' pupil Plato (428–347) dealt with some of the most profound issues of political philosophy, the theory of knowledge, and the nature of reality. He proposed an undemocratic utopian state (*The Republic*), which would be strictly ordered and ruled by philosopher kings.

d. *Aristotle:* Plato's pupil Aristotle (384–322) had encyclopedic interests. Most important, his approach was empirical, drawing generalizations from large numbers of facts and observations (*Politics, Ethics*).

GREEKS began to suspect that there was an order in the universe beyond manipulation by the gods - philosophy

II. The Rise of Macedonia

1. The Weaknesses of the Poleis

During the 300s, the Greek city-states—principally Athens, Thebes, and Sparta—struggled for dominance and factually weakened themselves.

In 394 BC. Athens Rebuilt Navy and herassed the seas/

2. Philip II of Macedonia

By 338, Philip II, through clever use of aggression and diplomacy, had led Macedonia to dominance over most of the important Greek city-states. In 336 he was assassinated.

3. Alexander the Great

Alexander carried out his father's plans to invade Persia. By the time of his death in 323, Alexander had defeated the decaying Persian Empire and established his rule from Egypt and Greece in the West to the Indus River in the East. Interpretations of his motives and efforts differ widely.

Alexanders Empire disintegrated at his Death Because He Did Not Designate an Hier./

III. The Hellenistic Age (323–130 B.C.E.)

1. The Dissolution of Alexander's Empire

Alexander's empire was carved up into three kingdoms and later a fourth in decades after his death. With Greeks usually holding the high offices, these efficiently run kingdoms were often at war with each other. Women sometimes reemerged as rulers.

2. Economic Life

In the Hellenistic world large estates predominated. Greeks brought new vigor to the economy. Long-distance trade flourished. The resulting prosperity, however, was unevenly distributed, leading to increasing social conflict.

The Hellenistic world prospered !

3. Hellenistic Cities

Cities of great size dominated Hellenistic civilization as centers of government, trade, and culture. There Greeks established temples, theaters, gymnasiums, and schools as Greek became an international language.

4. Literature, Art, and Science

Advanced scholarship, especially around the library in Alexandria, and professionalism marked the age. Architecture and sculpture became grandiose, emotional, and realistic (Altar of Zeus in Pergamum). Advances were made in mathematics and science that would not be surpassed for centuries (Euclid, geometry; Archimedes, mathematics, and physics; Aristarchus, mathematics and astronomy; Ptolemy, astronomy). *Archimedes calculated the value of π !*

5. Philosophy and Religion

Philosophy, mainly for the intellectual elite, was dominated by Epicureanism and Stoicism, both of which were individualistic. Epicurus (341–270) believed that people should avoid anxiety by leading pleasurable, tranquil lives. For the most part, this meant withdrawal and avoidance of physical and mental pain rather than self-indulgence. Zeno (335–263), and later the Stoics, emphasized universal brotherhood and the virtues of tolerance, patience in adversity, self-discipline, and justice toward the less fortunate members of the human race—a philosophy that was influential among Romans. For the masses, Eastern religious came to dominate, especially ritualistic and emotional mystery cults centering on the worship of a redeeming savior and deities such as Isis and Osiris.

GUIDE TO DOCUMENTS

Oedipus' Self-Mutilation

1. What psychological insights are revealed in this excerpt?
2. What, for the Greeks, might be the lessons to be learned from this tragedy?

Thucydides: The Melian Dialogue

1. Put into your own words, first, the argument of the Athenians and, second, the argument of the Melians.
2. What does this excerpt reveal about the nature of Athens and its empire?

Socrates Is Sentenced to Death

1. What was Socrates' attitude toward the jury and Athenians?
2. According to Socrates, what were the qualities of "the good man"?

SIGNIFICANT INDIVIDUALS

Political Leaders

Philip II (359–336), king of Macedonia.
Alexander III (336–323), king of Macedonia.

Darius III (336–330), king of Persia.

Dramatists

Aeschylus (525?–456), Athenian.
Sophocles (496?–406), Athenian.

Euripides (480?–406?), Athenian.
Aristophanes (448?–385?), Athenian.

Historians

Herodotus (484?–425?), Greek.

Thucydides (455?–399?), Athenian.

Philosophers

Thales of Miletus (625–ca. 546), scientist.
Anaximander of Miletus (611?–547?), astronomer.
Pythagoras of Samos (ca. 530), mathematician.
Protagoras (5th century), Greek Sophist.

Socrates (469–399), Athenian.
Plato (428–347), Athenian.
Aristotle (384–322), Athenian.
Zeno (333?–262), Greek.
Epicurus (341–270), Greek.

Astronomers

Aristarchus (3rd century), Greek.
Hipparchus (190?–after 126), Greek.

Eratosthenes (275?–194?), Greek.
Ptolemy of Alexandria (ca. C.E. 140), Greek.

Others

Demosthenes (384–322), Athenian
 orator.
Theocritus (3rd century), Greek poet.

Euclid (ca. 300), Greek geometer.
Archimedes (287?–212), Greek
 mathematician.

CHRONOLOGICAL DIAGRAM

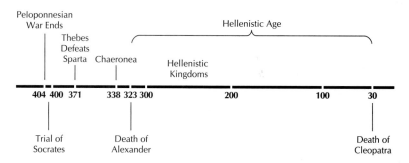

IDENTIFICATION

the *Oresteia*
Melian Dialogue
Sophists
Socratic method
The Republic

Idealism
Hellenization
Stoicism
Epicureanism
mystery cults

MAP EXERCISES

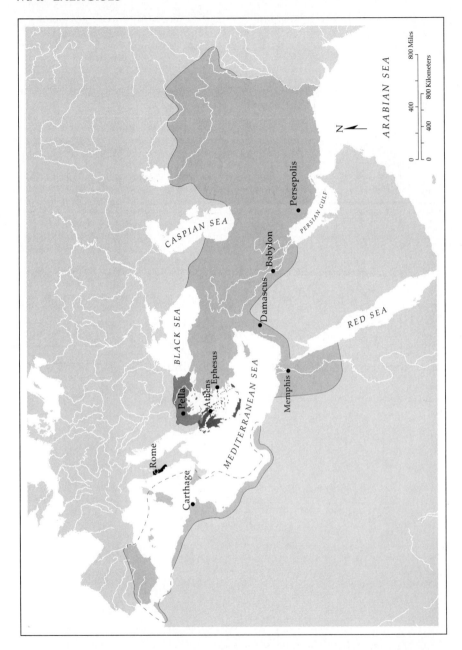

1. Indicate the areas controlled by Rome, Carthage, Egypt, Persia, the Greek city-states, and Macedonia aroun 340 B.C.E., prior to Alexander's conquests.
2. Indicate which of these civilizations is a rising power during this period and which is a declining power.

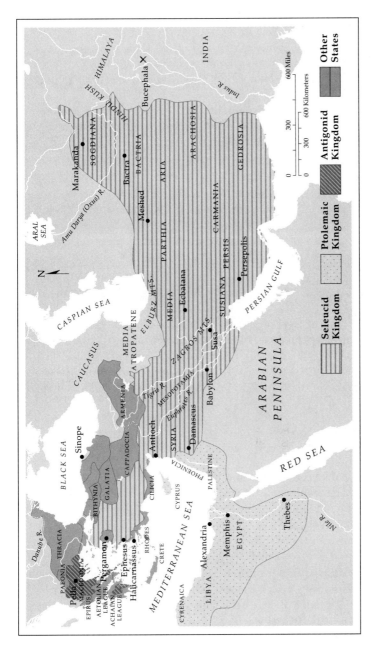

1. This map shows the Hellenistic world after Alexander's death. What does this reveal about the ability of Alexander's successors to hold his conquests together? What might this reveal about the mixing of cultures in this part of the world during the two centuries following Alexander's death?

PROBLEMS FOR ANALYSIS

I. *Classical Greek Culture*

1. In what ways does Greek drama reflect characteristics of Greek culture as well as universal human problems?
2. Trace the evolution of Greek philosophy from its beginnings in the seventh century B.C.E. to Aristotle in the fourth century B.C.E. What historical trends in Athenian life does this evolution reflect?

II. *The Rise of Macedonia*

1. "The Macedonian conquest of Greece was really a blessing in disguise." Do you agree? Explain.

III. *The Hellenistic Age*

1. Compare the Classical Age with the Hellenistic Age. What are the main differences?
2. How did the spread of Greeks into the East affect those areas? What were the economic and cultural consequences of Hellenization?
3. Some people argue that literature, art, science, and philosophy did not decline after the fourth century, but that they simply turned to other styles and concerns equal in quality to those of the earlier period. Do you agree?

SPECULATIONS

1. How does the civilization of fifth-and fourth-century Athens compare with our own? In which would you rather live? Why?
2. "Whether or not Alexander had high ideals behind his conquests, he and his followers should be praised, for they infused relatively backward civilizations with more advanced Greek institutions and ideals." Do you agree? Why?
3. "It is a mistake to be so admiring of the ancient Greeks. We think highly of their civilization only because it resembles our own in some ways, and we overlook the fact that it was based upon slave labor, the subjection of women, and almost perpetual warfare." Do you agree? Why?

TRANSITIONS

In "The Forming of Greek Civilization," the evolution of Greek civilization from Minoan and Mycenaean origins to the fifth-century war between Athens and Sparta was traced.

In "Classical and Hellenistic Greece," intellectual and artistic achievements of Classical Greece and the succeeding Hellenistic Age are examined. Politically, however, the Greek city-states declined. Philip II and Alexander the Great of Macedonia were able to conquer the Greeks. The victories of Alexander in the East led to the formation of powerful warring Hellenistic kingdoms, relative prosperity, and an expansion of Greek culture.

In "The Roman Republic," the development of Roman civilization through the first century B.C.E. will be traced. During this period political dominance over the Mediterranean will shift westward, the Romans ultimately conquering the various parts of the Hellenistic world while absorbing aspects of its culture.

FOUR
THE ROMAN REPUBLIC

MAIN THEMES

1. Through a number of long wars, a series of internal struggles, and a system of confederation, the Romans unified the Italian peninsula under their rule. Plebeians struggled with the long-dominant patricians for political power.
2. Wars and interventions in Africa, Spain, Greece, and Asia Minor made Rome the supreme Mediterranean power.
3. In their religion and culture, Romans were heavily influenced by the Greeks, but they developed their own rites and literature.
4. Between 133 and 31, Rome experienced a slow revolution marked by the rise of powerful men, such as Sulla, Pompey, and Julius Caesar, resulting in the fall of the Republic.
5. Octavian defeated his competitors, brought the Republic to an end, and established the structures of the Empire.

OUTLINE AND SUMMARY

From the beginning the theme of the Roman Republic was conquest and domination.

I. The Unification of Italy (to 264 B.C.E.)

1. The Geography of Italy

Mountains divide Italy into numerous valleys; the most fertile of these is around the Po River in the north.

2. Early Rome

Rome, forming about 625, was at first under the control of the already established Etruscans. The sophisticated Etruscan civilization, influenced by contact with the Greeks, flourished until the fourth century, when the Romans, who first freed themselves around 500, finally absorbed it. The Roman Republic was based on an unwritten constitution of customary laws. Although occasionally a temporary "dictator" was appointed, generally rule was divided between the elected magistrates (consuls), the Senate, and the assemblies. However, the family was the real location of power in Roman society.

3. The Struggle of the Orders (494–287 B.C.E.)

Roman citizens were divided into the patricians, an aristocratic order with a base of power in the Senate, and the plebeians, the majority, who had a right to vote in the assemblies. In a series of struggles, the plebeians gradually gained concessions from the patricians and acquired more influence over Roman political institutions. But for the most part the patricians managed to control changes.

4. Early Expansion of Rome

In a series of long and costly wars, sometimes marked by defeats, Rome gained control of the Italian peninsula by 265. Rome effectively administered conquered territory through a system of confederation, which allowed some communities full citizenship, others partial citizenship, and still others allied status.

II. The Age of Mediterranean Conquest (264–133 B.C.E.)

1. The Punic Wars

Between 264 and 146, three wars with Carthage, the major power in the western Mediterranean, established Rome as the dominant power there. The second Punic War (219–202) was the most significant, as Rome, led by Scipio, defeated Hannibal and took over most of Carthage's territories. In the third Punic War (149–146), Rome destroyed Carthage.

2. Expansion in the Eastern Mediterranean

Rome became involved in wars against Macedonia and then expanded further east. By 133 Rome had annexed Macedonia and Greece and had obtained the Kingdom of Pergamum.

3. The Nature of Roman Expansion

Through a policy of forming alliances, mastering military force, and expanding ruthlessly, Rome came to dominate the Mediterranean.

    a. *Provincial Administration:* The Senate appointed provincial governors with almost absolute powers. Usually their rule was effective; taxes from the provinces supported Rome.

4. Roman Society in the Republic

    a. *The Roman Family:* The father was considered the absolute owner of the whole family, women were praised above all for their obedience and domestic virtues. Over time, women gained greater freedom, cultural prominence, and behind-the-scenes political importance.

    b. *Religion:* Within Roman households, the father acted as a priest in the worship of household gods. Public religion was closely connected with the interests of the state. The Romans adapted Greek mythology, giving Greek deities Roman names.

c.   *Early Roman Literature:* The Romans, mostly influenced by Greek literature, eventually developed their own Latin literature. Dramatists (Plautus and Terence) wrote comedies based on the Greek New Comedy. The Greek Polybius helped create a Roman literary tradition as historian of the Hellenistic Age and early Roman history.

III.   The Roman Revolution (133–27 B.C.E.)

1.   Social Change and the Gracchi

a.   *The Changing World of Italy:* The wars with Carthage impoverished the Italian peasantry, and slaves depressed workers' wages, weakening recruitment for Rome's armies.

b.   *Tiberius Gracchus:* In 133 Tiberius sponsored policies of land redistribution from the rich to the poor. Some senators arranged for his assassination.

c.   *Gaius Gracchus:* In 123 Gaius proposed measures to elevate the equestrians (a middle class) to greater political power. The Senate turned against him, but a pattern of demagogues struggling for power had been initiated as had the slow Roman revolution.

2.   The Years of the Warlords

Struggles among powerful generals undermined the Republic.

a.   *Marius:* Gaius Marius gained great stature as a successful general and created an army that for the first time included the poor and volunteers. He thus solved some of the problems of displaced farmers and recruitment, while also creating an army rewarded by and loyal to its commander.

b.   *The War with the Italians:* Through wars between 91 and 88 B.C.E., Italian allies of Rome gained citizenship.

c.   *Senatorial Reaction under Sulla:* After a civil war broke out, the Roman general Sulla conquered Rome in 82, became dictator, instituted political and legal reforms to bring back the power and prestige of the Senate, and then resigned from office.

d.   *The Rise of Pompey:* Pompey, through successful campaigns from Spain in the West to Syria in the East, succeeded Sulla as Rome's most powerful general. As consul with Crassus, he canceled several of Sulla's arrangements.

e.   *Cicero:* Cicero became an important nonmilitary statesman and the most versatile Latin writer of his time. In politics, he hoped that harmony between the senatorial and equestrian classes would preserve the traditional constitution.

3.   The First Triumvirate

In 59 Julius Caesar, returning from Spain, combined with Pompey and the wealthy Crassus to form the First Triumvirate, which further weakened the power and prestige of the Senate. Between 58 and 50 Caesar expanded Roman territories by conquering Gallic tribes in modern France and Belgium.

4.   *The Supremacy of Julius Caesar*

a.   *The Break between Caesar and the Senate:*   In 49 a faction of the Senate, fearing Caesar might destroy the Roman constitution, tried to strip Caesar to his command and turn Pompey against him.

b.   *Caesar's Invasion of Italy:*   Challenged by the Senate, Caesar successfully invaded Italy and then decisively defeated Pompey in Greece.

c.   *Caesar's Rule to 44 B.C.E.:*   Caesar made himself dictator for life, instituted a series of reforms, and turned the Senate into his rubber stamp.

d.   *The Death of Caesar:*   In 44 Caesar was murdered by aristocratic conspirators led by Brutus and Cassius. This controversial man's career reveals the political weakness of the late Roman Republic.

IV.   *The End of the Roman Republic*

1.   *The Second Triumvirate*

Despite attempts by senators to reassert republican government, Octavian, Marc Antony, and Lepidus formed the Second Triumvirate in 43 and, after defeating Brutus and Cassius, ruled for a number of years. Ultimately, the two major partners, Antony and Octavian, struggled for power. Octavian defeated Antony in 31. The following year Antony and Cleopatra took their lives before Octavian could capture them in Egypt, marking an end to the Hellenistic Age.

V.   *The Founding of the Roman Empire*

1.   *Augustus and the Principate*

Though appearing to return power to the Senate, Octavian actually turned the Republic into an Empire. He took direct command of vast provinces, established his system (the Principate), and had his name changed to Augustus.

2.   *Augustus, the First Roman Emperor*

Augustus laid foundations for the deification of emperors. He solidified frontiers and created an elite security force—the Praetorian Guard. His rule was marked by relative peace, prosperity, and cultural creativity. He formed the structure of the Roman Empire.

GUIDE TO DOCUMENTS

The Murder of Julius Caesar

1. In this account of the murder of Julius Caesar, what impression is the author, Plutarch, trying to create in the minds of readers?

2. What does this reveal about the problems facing the Senate in these last years of the Roman Republic?

SIGNIFICANT INDIVIDUALS

Political and Military Leaders

Hannibal (247–183), Carthaginian general.

Gaius Gracchus (153–121), Roman statesman, tribune.

Gaius Marius (157–86), Roman general.

Lucius Cornelius Sulla (138–78), Roman general, dictator.

Pompey (106–48), general, consul.

Marcus Licinius Crassus (115?–53), general, consul.

Gaius Julius Caesar (100–44), general, consul, dictator.

Marc Antony (83?–30), consul, tribune, soldier.

Octavian (Augustus) (63 B.C.E.– C.E. 14), consul, emperor.

Cleopatra (51–49, 48–30), queen of Egypt.

Writers

Quintus Ennius (239–169), Latin writer.

Lucretius (94–55), Latin poet.

Polybius (200?–118?), Greek historian.

Marcus Tullius Cicero (106–43), Latin writer, politician.

CHRONOLOGICAL DIAGRAM

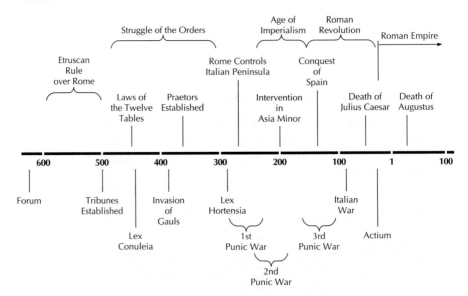

IDENTIFICATION

consul
Senate
Struggle of the Orders
tribune
Lex Canuleia
equestrians

Italian War
Tribal Assembly
amicitia
First Triumvirate
Actium

MAP EXERCISES

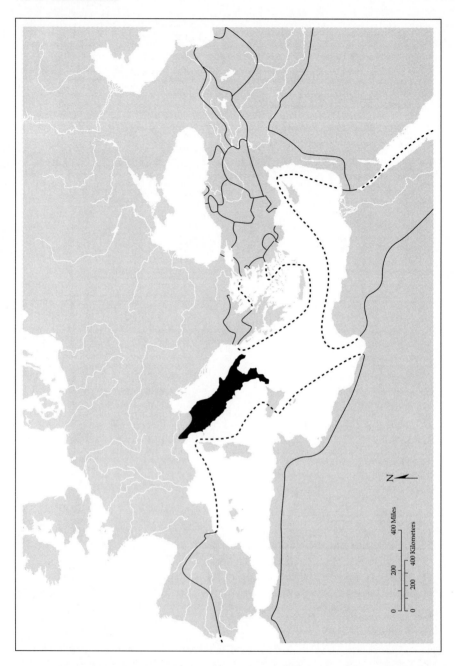

1. Label the main political powers of the Mediterranean basin around 264 B.C.E.

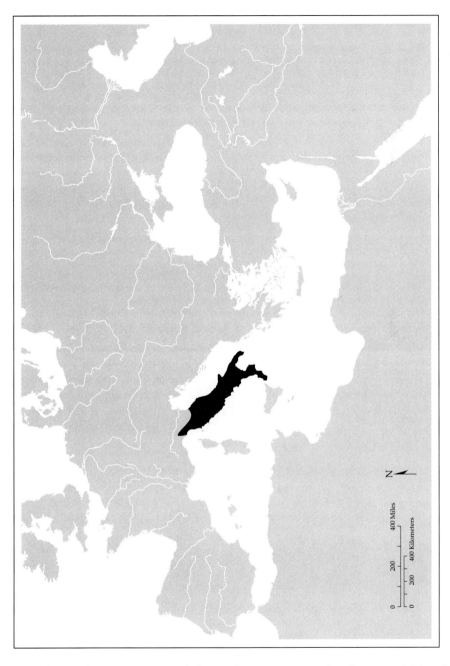

1. Indicate the main areas and dates of Roman expansion between 264 and
   44 B.C.E. Compare this map and the previous map. At whose expense did
   Rome expand during this period?

PROBLEMS FOR ANALYSIS

I. The Unification of Italy

1. Polybius called the Roman constitution a perfect blend of regal, aristocratic, and democratic elements. Do you agree? Explain.
2. How were the Romans able to hold their growing territories together during the early period of the Roman Republic?

II. The Age of Mediterranean Conquest

1. Trace the main steps by which Rome became an imperial power. What role did Rome's system of alliances and its method of provincial administration play in this?
2. What was the nature of Roman society, religion, and culture? What connections might be drawn between the three?

III. The Roman Revolution

1. What were the fundamental strains and changes that undermined the foundations of the Roman Republic? How is this reflected in the developments concerning Tiberius and Gaius Gracchus?
2. What role did powerful generals play in the decline of the Republic? Use examples.
3. How did the Senate respond to threats? Did it simply give up, respond in kind, or pursue policies that further undermined its own authority?

IV. The End of the Roman Republic

1. How was Octavian able to acquire supreme power over his competitors?
2. In what ways did Octavian's victory mark the end of the Roman Republic and the Hellenistic Age?

V. The Founding of the Roman Empire

1. What policies did Augustus follow to secure his own power and establish the structure of the Roman Empire?

SPECULATIONS

1. Suppose you were a Roman. Present arguments justifying Roman expansion as something more than ruthless territorial acquisition.
2. What policies should the Senate have followed to prevent the fall of the Roman Republic? Do you think it would have been better if the Republic had been preserved? Explain.
3. Compare the strengths and weaknesses of the Greeks and Romans.

TRANSITIONS

In "Classical and Hellenistic Greece," Greek civilization at its height as well as its spread and transformation in the East under Alexander and his successors were examined.

In "The Roman Republic," the Romans—driven by a desire to impose themselves on all others, supported by large reserves of manpower, and aided by an authoritarian view of life—succeeded in unifying most of the Mediterranean and European worlds under their rule. In the latter years of the Republic a revolution eliminated political freedom. Years of instability were finally brought to an end by Octavian, who effectively established the Roman Empire.

In "The Empire and Christianity," the Roman Empire as its height, the growth of a new religion (Christianity), and the transformation and decline of the Empire will be examined.

FIVE
THE EMPIRE
AND CHRISTIANITY

MAIN THEMES

1. Thanks to an effective government, a well-functioning corps of civil servants, and a generally reliable defense force, the two centuries after the death of Augustus were a period of relative peace, prosperity, and creative accomplishment.
2. In the third century the Empire experienced political instability, economic decline, social turmoil, and cultural disintegration.
3. Although reforms by Diocletian and Constantine extended the life of the Empire, the Western Empire succumbed to a number of problems and fell—marking a turning point in history.
4. Despite opposition from the government and from heretical divisions, the Christian Church formulated dogma and became established, effecting a cultural revolution in the Classical world.

OUTLINE AND SUMMARY

After two centuries of peace and prosperity, the Empire experienced a long crisis and, in the West, decline. But a new set of religious beliefs—Christianity—was being established.

I. The Empire at Its Height

Three unifying elements made the Empire survive and work: the figure of the emperor, the civil servants and the city councils, and the army.

1. The Successors of Augustus

The Julio-Claudian emperors who succeeded Augustus until C.E. 68 were of low quality but managed to keep power and the peace. The Praetorian Guard started intervening in civil authority.

2. The Five Good Emperors

From the end of the first century to the end of the second century, five capable emperors ruled Rome. Trajan led Rome to its furthest extension to the east in 116. During this period of prosperity, vast building projects were undertaken.

3. Roman Imperial Civilization

a. *Economy:* During the late Republic and early Empire, Romans enjoyed extraordinary prosperity. Cities, smaller in the West (except for Rome), were of great importance as centers of commerce, manufacturing, government, and culture. At least 75 percent of the Empire's total product remained agricultural. In Italy, and to a lesser extent elsewhere, the great slave-run estates (*latifundia*) replaced the small farm. They specialized in the cultivation of vines, olives, and fruit; raised livestock; and provided cities with wood and stone. Provincial areas started to threaten Italy's economic leadership.

b. *Social Conditions:* The rich led luxurious lives of indulgence, especially compared to the workers and the poor. Yet workers had better working conditions than had existed in earlier times, and the poor, who made up some 50 percent of the city's population, were supported at public expense. In general, social mobility became easier within the Empire, and ultimately men from the provinces entered all Roman institutions.

c. *Law:* The development of an evolving, respected legal system was one of Rome's greatest cultural accomplishments. The legal system was divided into laws applying to citizens ("civil law") and laws applying to foreigners (law of other nations).

d. *Engineering and Architecture:* The Romans were superb engineers and architects. They built long-lasting roads, aqueducts, baths, forums, temples, and public halls throughout the Empire. By using arches on a large scale and by inventing concrete, the Romans were able to build on a scale far beyond that of the Greeks.

e. *Literature in the Empire:* Poetry was popular in Rome among the upper classes. The most famous poets—Virgil (*Aeneid*), Horace (*Odes*), and Ovid—often borrowed from Greek models.

f. *Historians:* During the Republic most histories were written by men involved in politics. In the early years of the Empire, Livy wrote an ambitious, rhetorical, but questionable history of Rome (*Roman History*). Tacitus (*Histories, Annals*) was Rome's greatest historian, emphasizing character analysis.

II. Changes in Ancient Society

1. The Period of Crisis (192–284)

After the death of Emperor Commodus in 192, a series of ineffective emperors took the throne and the army became undisciplined. The weakness of the Senate and an unwillingness of talented people to hold public office lowered the quality of the administration. The economy was burdened by high costs (defense, financial relief for the poor) and inflation.

a. *Slavery and its Dilemmas:* Slavery in Roman society was widespread and highly organized. In the long run, however, slavery weakened the economy, thereby contributing to the decline of the Empire in the West.

b. *The Plight of the Poor:* Toward the end of the Republic, the poor increasingly fled to the cities, especially to Rome, where they were supported.

Large areas of land became depopulated; policy toward the free cultivators (the coloni) indicates efforts both to encourage cultivation of abandoned lands and to tax them heavily as a needed source of revenue.

2. Cultural Disintegration

The cultural system of Classical antiquity appealed primarily to the elite, but left the poor largely ignored. Moreover there was a decline of creativity and a sense of pessimism plaguing most thinkers.

III. The Late Roman Empire

1. Restoration and Reform

In 284 Diocletian rose to power and brought order to the Empire by forming the Tetrarchy (rule of four). He imposed a more authoritarian, bureaucratic rule and reformed taxation. After a period of instability, he was succeeded by another strong emperor, Constantine, who in 330 established his capital in Constantinople (Byzantium).

2. Constantine and the Bureaucracy

Constantine cast the state into a rigid structure. The economy stagnated, and professions were made hereditary.

3. The Decline of the Western Empire

Emperors proved unable to hold the Empire together, and it was formally divided in half in 395. The Western portion declined as people became bound to their occupations and commerce declined. Large estates (villas) became more economically and then politically and militarily self-sufficient. By 476 the Empire ended in the West, but would survive in the East for another thousand years. There are numerous interpretations of the decline of the Western Empire. It was probably caused by a combination of factors. The West suffered from manpower shortages. It was more open geographically to invasion by warlike tribes, and it was militarily weakened by decentralization. The rigidity, the repression, and the welfare policies of Rome may have made its people particularly apathetic. Christianity may also have weakened the defenses of the Empire.

IV. Christianity and Its Early Rivals

The triumph of Christianity was a remarkable cultural revolution.

1. The Mystery Religions

Mystery religions, offering a blessed life after death to the initiated, spread through the Empire. Christianity, strongly associated with Judaism, differed in important ways from other mystery religions.

2. The Jews in the Roman Empire

With the exception of one main period (164–63 B.C.E.) the Jews were directly or indirectly governed by outside rulers. Despite attempts at repression, Judaism retained its coherence and strength.

a. *Jewish Factions:* After the Maccabean Revolt (167–164 B.C.E.) Jews were divided into three main factions: the Sadducees, the Pharisees, and the Essenes. Some argue that the Essenes were related to the first Christians.

3. Origins of Christianity

From a historical perspective, it is difficult to know much about the life of Jesus. According to accounts in the New Testament written decades after his death, Jesus offered salvation to the deserving and encouraged followers to perform rituals and form a community. The movement became all-inclusive.

a. *Paul and His Mission:* Paul converted to Christianity and organized Christian communities of Jews and gentiles throughout the Roman world. In his influential writings, Paul established the Christian Church on the basis of personal faith. His message emphasizing Jesus as a founder, restorer, and redeemer in a new messianic age brought many converts to the new Church.

b. *Persecutions:* Christians, like Jews, set themselves apart by refusing to worship Roman gods. Sporadic persecutions were sometimes carried out (especially under Diocletian, 303–313) but failed, merely creating a list of venerated Christian martyrs.

c. *An Emperor Becomes the Church's Patron:* In 313 Constantine extended freedom of worship to the Christians and granted the Church privileged status. In 391 Theodosius made Christianity the state religion, outlawing all others.

4. Battles within Christianity

a. *Dogma and Heresies:* Heretical movements within Christianity (Marcion, Montanus) stimulated the Church to define its dogma.

b. *The Government of the Church:* During the first and second centuries, the administrative structure of the church was developed. At first, women often served in leading positions, but later, their role was limited. Eventually the bishop of Rome became head (*pope*) of the Church in the West.

c. *Donatists and Arians:* Donatists, based in North Africa, created a schism by insisting that sacraments administered by "corrupt" priests were not valid. Arians, arguing that Jesus and God were not of the same substance, were condemned at the Nicene Council in 325.

d. *The Church and Classical Culture:* Christians found it necessary to learn pagan intellectual skills and turn them to their own purposes, preserving much of Classical literature in the process.

5. The Fathers of the Church

The Fathers of the early Church, working through the languages and thought of Greco-Roman civilization, wrote a vast amount of authoritative commentary, persuasion, and teaching. The most important of these were the Greek fathers Origen and Eusebius of Caesarea and the Latin fathers Ambrose and Jerome.

a. *Augustine:* Augustine, the best known of the fathers, commented on almost every question of Christian theology, including sexual morality and marriage. In his *Confessions* he revealed his own spiritual progress. As bishop of Hippo he defended the traditional Church against Pelagius, arguing that grace and not just good works is necessary for salvation. He emphasized God's omnipotence and man's helplessness. In his masterpiece, *The City of God,* he described an order in history directed by God and emphasized the City of God (for the elect).

GUIDE TO DOCUMENTS

Tacitus on the Powers of Augustus

1. What, according to Tacitus, explains Augustus' acquisition of such great power?
2. What does this reveal about the state of government prior to this acquisition of power by Augustus?

Augustine Is Brought to His Faith

1. What insights might this excerpt provide concerning the conversion of Augustine?
2. How does this conversion relate to some of the later doctrines favored by Augustine, such as those related to sex and renunciation?
3. How might this explain some of the appeal of Christianity?

SIGNIFICANT INDIVIDUALS

Emperors

Augustus (Octavian) (27 B.C.E.–C.E. 14)

Diocletian (284–305)
Constantine (306–337)

Writers

Virgil (70–19), Latin poet.
Horace (65–8), Latin poet.
Juvenal (C.E. 60?–C.E. 140), Latin poet, satirist.

Livy (59 B.C.E.–C.E. 17), historian.
Cornelius Tacitus (55?–120?), historian.

Religious Leaders

Paul (1st century C.E.), Church founder.

Montanus (ca. 150–200), bishop, Montanist leader.

Origen (185?–255?), Greek Church father.

Eusebius of Caesarea (260?–340?), Greek Church father.

Ambrose of Milan (340?–397), Latin Church father.

Jerome (340?–420), Latin Church father.

Augustine of Hippo (354-430), Latin Church father.

Pelagius (360?–420?), Irish monk, theologian.

CHRONOLOGICAL DIAGRAM

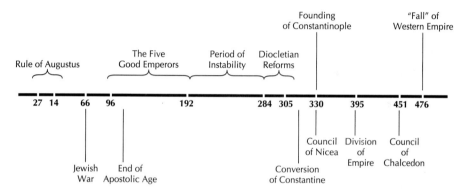

IDENTIFICATION

latifundia
public games
jurists
ius civile
Roman baths
Pompeii
coloni
mystery religions

Essenes
persecutions
conversion of Constantine
Gnostics
Nicene Creed
The City of God
Diocletian reforms

MAP EXERCISES

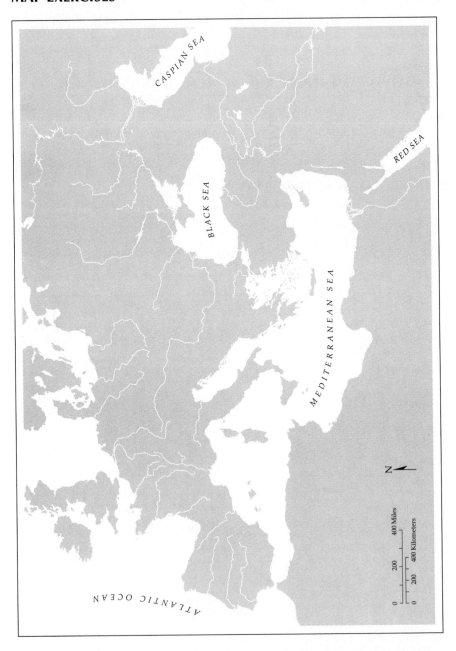

1. Indicate the outlines of the Empire in C.E. 14 and its subsequent maximum expansion.
2. Indicate the geographic expansion of Christianity around the year 312.

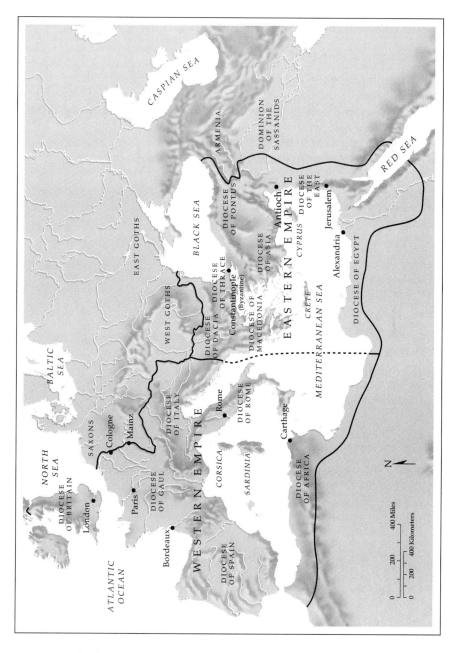

1. During the fourth century the Roman Empire was divided into Western and Eastern halves. Considering that many of the invaders came from the north and northeast, what geographical factors help explain the vulnerability of the West compared to that of the East?
2. How might this division of the Roman Empire relate to the later division between the Byzantine Empire and medieval Western Europe?

PROBLEMS FOR ANALYSIS

I. The Empire at Its Height

1. Analyze the way in which the socioeconomic system of the Empire functioned. What were its economic characteristics? What role did slaves play economically and socially? How sharp were economic and social distinctions between rich and poor?
2. Historians argue that Romans were most skilled in law, engineering, and architecture. Using examples, support this argument.

II. Changes in Ancient Society

1. While in the short run slavery as an economic system worked well, in the long run it worked to the disadvantage of the Empire. Explain.
2. Analyze the crisis of the third century. How is this reflected in the cultural disintegration of the period?

III. The Late Roman Empire

1. What problems did the reforms of Diocletian and Constantine solve, and what new problems did they create?
2. Considering the variety of interpretations, explain the causes for the decline of the Roman Empire in the West.

IV. Christianity and Its Early Rivals

1. Analyze the similarities and differences of Christianity and other mystery religions. What characteristics of Christianity contributed to its success?
2. How did theological controversies contribute to establishing Christian dogma and order within the Church?

SPECULATIONS

1. As an early leader of the Christian Church, what policies should you follow to ensure the spread of a single Christian religion? Why?
2. What might Roman emperors have done to prevent the fall of the Empire in the West?
3. Hold a debate between representatives of a pagan Classical culture and a Christian culture. Indicate the main points and responses each would make.

TRANSITIONS

In "The Roman Republic," the rise of Rome as a world power was traced. The period ended with the fall of the Republic and the establishment of the Empire by Augustus.

In "The Empire and Christianity," the story begins with the period just after the establishment of the Empire by Augustus. For about two centuries the Empire prospered, but during the third century a long series of crises occurred, eventually breaking apart the Empire and leading to its final collapse in the West during the fifth century. Numerous factors—including profound flaws in the slave economy, conflicting values, and changes in all sectors of life—weakened the Empire, causing it to decline. Yet at the same time people were laying the basis for a new civilization, above all by building on the legacy of Rome and spreading a new set of religious beliefs—Christianity.

In "The Making of Western Europe," the development of a new civilization in the West between the fifth and tenth centuries will be traced.

SECTION SUMMARY
THE ANCIENT WORLD TO C.E. 500
CHAPTERS 1–5

CHRONOLOGICAL DIAGRAMS

Diagram 1
The Ancient Civilizations

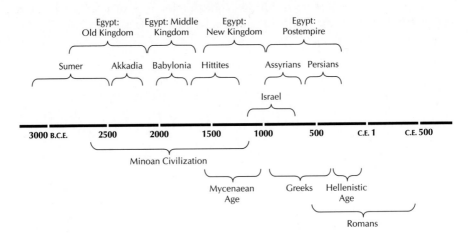

Diagram 2
Greco-Roman Civilization

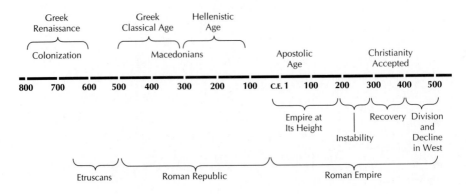

MAP EXERCISES

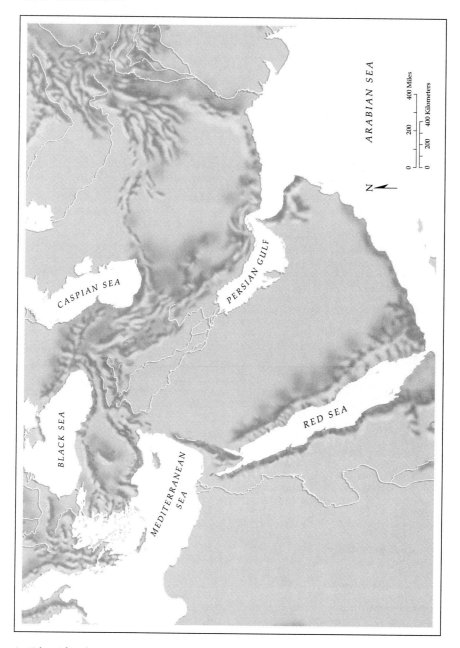

1. Identify the centers and the approximate boundaries of the following civilizations:
   a. Babylonia, 1900 B.C.E.
   b. Egypt, 1300 B.C.E.
   c. Israel, 900 B.C.E.
   d. Persia, 500 B.C.E.
   e. Minoan and Mycenaean, 1400 B.C.E.
   f. Greece, 400 B.C.E.
   g. Hellenistic Kingdoms, 250 B.C.E.

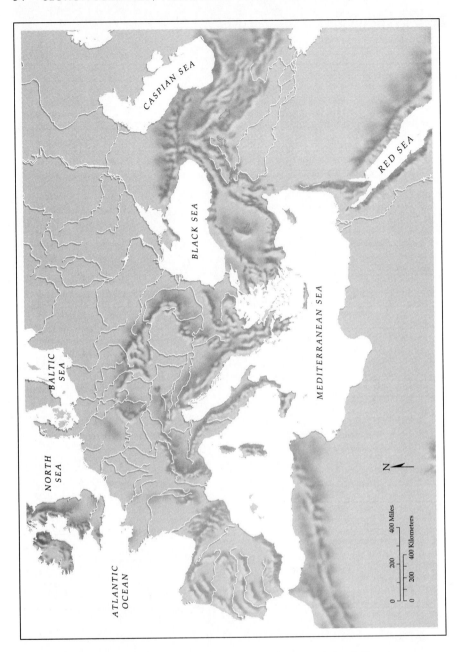

1. Identify the centers and approximate boundaries of the following:
   a. Rome, 250 B.C.E.
   b. Rome, 50 B.C.E.
   c. Rome, C.E. 150
   d. The Eastern and Western Roman Empires, fourth century.

BOX CHART

Reproduce the Box Chart in a larger format in your notebook or on a separate sheet of paper.

Rome	Greece	Egypt	Mesopotamia Near East	
				Chronological Divisions
				Political Institutions and Developments
				Economic System and Characteristics
				Social System and Characteristics
				Religious System and Characteristics
				Cultural Values and Productions
				Problems
				Political Leaders
				Religious Leaders
				Philosophers and Scientists
				Cultural Leaders
				Others
				Turning Points

SIX
THE MAKING
OF WESTERN EUROPE

MAIN THEMES

1. "Barbarian" peoples invaded Roman territories, merging their own institutions and culture with those of the declining Roman civilization.
2. Commerce and industry decreased, and Europe became a peasant society organized around the single-family farm and a central manor.
3. The Christian Church, through the growth of the Roman papacy and monasticism, maintained Roman traditions of social order and Classical culture.
4. The Franks and Anglo-Saxons created temporarily effective kingdoms.
5. The Church and scholars of the Carolingian Renaissance helped preserve Classical learning.

OUTLINE AND SUMMARY

I. *The New Community of Peoples*

The civilization that was the direct ancestor of the modern Western world took shape during the Middle Ages (500–1500) in the west and north of Europe. It was founded upon a new community composed of former Roman subjects and "barbarians."

1. *The Great Migrations*

Celtic, Germanic, and Slavic tribes bordered the Roman Empire to the north and east. In the fourth and fifth centuries, Germanic tribes, pressured by population growth and by Huns from the East, successfully invaded Roman territories in great numbers. Visigoths were followed by Vandals, Burgundians, Franks, Ostrogoths, Angles, Saxons, and Jutes. Each took different routes of conquest, establishing themselves from Britain to North Africa with varying amounts of permanence and organization. Most important were the Visigoths, who were the first to decisively defeat the Romans (378) and establish an autonomous kingdom on Roman soil (418); the Ostrogoths, who formally took over Italy from the last roman emperor (476); and the Franks, who, under Clovis (481–511), unified Gaul and converted to Roman Christianity.

In the fifth and sixth centuries, Slavic tribes penetrated into eastern and south-eastern Europe to become ancestors of modern peoples in those areas.

2.   Germans and Romans

Germans constituted a minority of the population within the Roman Empire. They assimilated into Roman culture while also furthering the trend away from urban life toward that of small peasant villages and rural estates.

3.   Germanic Society

   a.   *The Role of Women:*   Women apparently had a higher status in Germanic society than in Roman society, probably because of their valued economic role. Germanic children, although not subject to infanticide as in Roman society, were poorly educated and treated with considerable neglect.

   b.   *Social Structure:*   Germanic society was based on individual ownership of land, bonds of blood relationship, and associations of self-help such as the *comitatus* and the guild. Kings rose during the invasions, but they were primarily only military and religious leaders.

   c.   *Law and Procedures:*   Legal decisions were based on recalled customs rather than written laws. Legal practices included publicly performed symbolic acts, use of witnesses, and use of juries. Councils or assemblies helped chiefs make decisions. Many of these institutions foreshadowed later medieval institutions.

   d.   *Germanic Culture:*   Since most Germans lacked writing skills, they preserved their literature orally. Their poetry typically glorified heroic military values (*Beowulf*). Germanic religion was magical and supernatural. Their most stunning artistic form was their animal style jewelry. The Germans combined with the masses of Roman subjects to strengthen this nonliterate culture.

II.   The New Economy, 500–900

In the Early Middle Ages, Europe became a peasant society built around the single-family farm.

1.   Agriculture

The climate and soil of northern Europe required new methods for successful cultivation. Slowly, these were developed during the Middle Ages through the use of heavier plows, more oxen and horses, improved harnesses, and better crop rotation (the three-field system). As a result, northern Europe was able to support a more dense population.

2.   The Manor

The manor was a tightly disciplined community of peasants organized under the authority of a lord. Characteristic of only certain areas, it became a fundamental unit of economic, political and social organization. It was almost self-sufficient. The lord was responsible for defense, law and order, and the administration of justice. He collected revenues from various monopolies (milling, brewing, salt), taxes, fixed-service obligations from his serfs, and produce from his own lands. Serfs and independent peasants had their own lands and rights to common pasture, which were protected by custom and morals.

3. The Exchange of Wealth

An "economy of gift and pillage," based on an ethic of reciprocal gift giving, replaced the market economy of Rome and helped tie together early medieval society. By the seventh century, commerce and industry had almost disappeared in the West, probably resulting from a lack of skills and interest.

III. The Leadership of the Church

The Church preserved Roman traditions of social order and Classical culture.

1. Origins of the Papacy

The early bishops of Rome gained a reputation as defenders of orthodoxy. This, the centrality of Rome, and biblical tradition probably combined to make the bishops of Rome the leaders of the Church. Supported by emperors and councils, popes gained authority, but not administrative dominance, in the fifth century. Gregory I (589–604)—by becoming the most effective leader in Rome, by managing Church estates, and by mounting effective missionary efforts in England and Spain—widened the authority of the Roman papacy and set a pattern for his successors.

2. Monasticism

Monasticism was first founded in Egypt in the third century. In the sixth century St. Benedict brought order and uniformity to this ascetic movement. The Benedictine rule granted authority to the abbot, instructed monks in practical and spiritual matters, and required them to do some manual labor. Monks, probably because of their communal organization and asceticism, became extremely important in medieval society. They supported local economic and social structures; served as teachers, advisers, and role models; promoted agriculture and savings; and supported new values in a difficult age.

IV. The New Political Structures

1. The Frankish Empire

Clovis' Merovingian successors were relatively weak, and thus power gravitated to a line of palace mayors. One of these mayors, Pepin the Short, gained support of aristocrats and Church officials and had himself recognized as king (751). He dignified his monarchy with Christian and Roman influences. Meanwhile, Frankish society was dividing into an aristocracy of warriors who could afford horses (a tremendous military advantage, thanks to the introduction of the stirrup) and of full-time peasants who could not.

a. *Charlemagne:* Pepin's son, Charlemagne (768–814), conquered vast territories, built up a Frankish Empire, and spread Christianity wherever he went. In 800 Pope Leo III crowned him emperor, symbolically marking the political and cultural autonomy of the West.

b. *Government:* A grandiose imperial ideology developed around Charlemagne, increasing his dignity. He governed with the help of court officials and local county administrators (counts). He further secured his own authority by traveling extensively, appointing traveling inspectors, and calling yearly general assemblies of notables.

c. *Decline of the Empire:* Charlemagne's successors were unable to hold the empire together. Central government became less effective, enabling counts and aristocrats to gain hereditary independence.

2. Renewed Invasions

In the ninth century Charlemagne's empire was invaded by the Saracens from the south, the Magyars from the east, and Vikings from the north. The Vikings were the most successful, their ships taking them from England and Spain in the West, to Russia and Constantinople in the East. By 1000, however, these new groups became Christianized partners in the association of Western peoples.

3. Anglo-Saxon England

England was unified religiously during the seventh century by the reforms of the archbishop of Canterbury, who built upon a variety of earlier missionary efforts. Political unity took longer, with various kings acquiring partial or complete authority between the seventh and ninth centuries.

a. *Alfred the Great:* Alfred (871–899) succeeded against the invading Danes and became England's first effective king. He initiated a cultural revival that included the beginnings of the *Anglo-Saxon Chronicle*. His successors retained power for about a century. There followed a period of instability and rule by Danish kings until the Norman Conquest in 1066.

V. Letters and Learning

Classical learning just barely survived and was used to promote the interests of the Christian religion.

1. The Church and Classical Learning

The Church was always committed to some learning, for the Bible and other religious texts had to be read and interpreted. In the fifth and sixth centuries, Christian scholars such as Boethius produced textbooks, translations, and compendiums of Classical learning. In addition, scholars—such as Pope Gregory (*Moralia in job, Dialogues*) and Gregory of Tours (*History of the Franks*)—

produced original books. When scholarship on the continent sank in the seventh century, Irish and English scholars, such a Bede the Venerable (*Ecclesiastical History of the English People*), carried on the Latin tradition. Most of this literature was filled with accounts of miracles, reflecting an assumption that the universe was shaped by miraculous interventions of God.

2.   The Carolingian Renaissance

Pepin, Charlemagne, and their successors energetically promoted learning to encourage religious uniformity and improve the supply of learned officials. Educational reforms were instituted, more efficient handwriting (the Carolingian minuscule) was created, scholarly language was made common (Medieval Latin), and important texts were standardized. These accomplishments revived mastery of correct Latin, led to a freer development of separate but related vernacular languages, and made possible future renaissances in Western thought.

GUIDE TO DOCUMENTS

Tacitus on the Early Germans

1. What evidence does this provide for the nature of Germanic politics?
2. What principles and practices governed the Germanic legal system?

Einhard on Charlemagne

1. From this evidence, what conclusions might be drawn about Charlemagne's personality?
2. How might one evaluate the objectivity of this description of Charlemagne? Does the author, Einhard, reveal any biases?

Charlemagne Imposes Christianity on the Saxons

1. What sorts of problems facing early Christianity are revealed by this document?
2. What sorts of beliefs and actions competed with Christian beliefs and actions?

SIGNIFICANT INDIVIDUALS

Political Leaders

Attila (433?–453), Hun.   Theodoric (474–526), Ostrogoth.
Odoacer (476–493), Germanic.   Clovis (481–511), Frank.

Charles Martel (715–741),
  Frank
Pepin the Short (751–768),
  Carolingian.

Charlemagne (768–814),
  Carolingian.
Alfred (871–899), Saxon.
Canute (1016–1035), Dane.

Religious Leaders

Gregory the Great (590–604),
  pope.

St. Benedict (480?–543?), monastic
  leader.

Cultural Figures

Tacitus (55?–120?), Roman
  historian.
Einhard (770?–840), Frankish
  biographer.
Boethius (480?–524?), Italian scholar.

Bede the Venerable (673?–735),
  English scholar.
Alcuin of York (735–804),
  English scholar.

CHRONOLOGICAL DIAGRAM

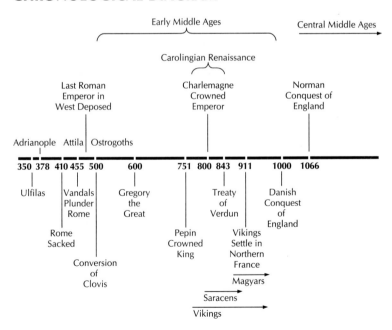

IDENTIFICATION

Celts

Gauls

Franks

Slavs

vulgar culture

Wergeld

the animal style

heavy plow

three-field system

manor

papal primacy

Benedictine rule

stirrup

county

missi dominici

Danegeld

standardized curriculum

Carolingian minuscule

Medieval Latin

MAP EXERCISES

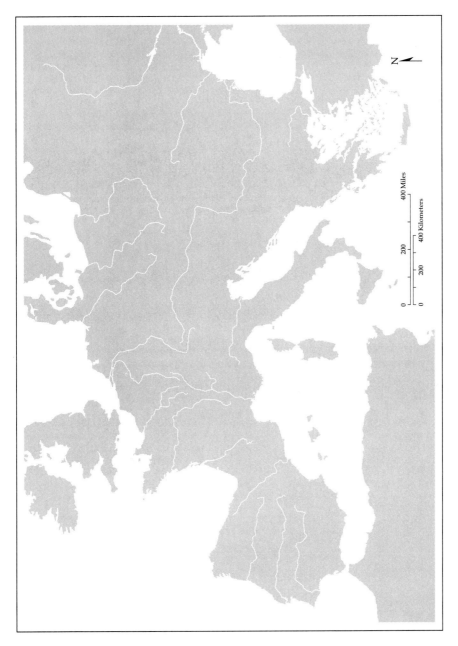

1. Indicate the areas where the Vandals, Visigoths, Franks, Anglo-Saxons, Burgundians, Alemanni, and Ostrogoths settled.

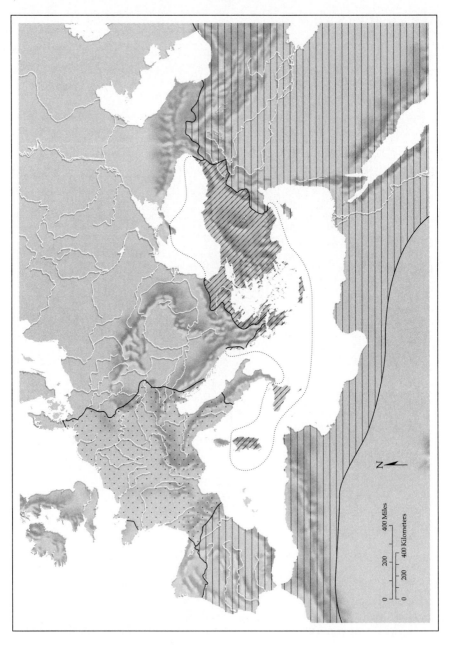

1. Label, around the year 800, the Frankish Empire under Charlemagne, the Byzantine Empire, and Islam.

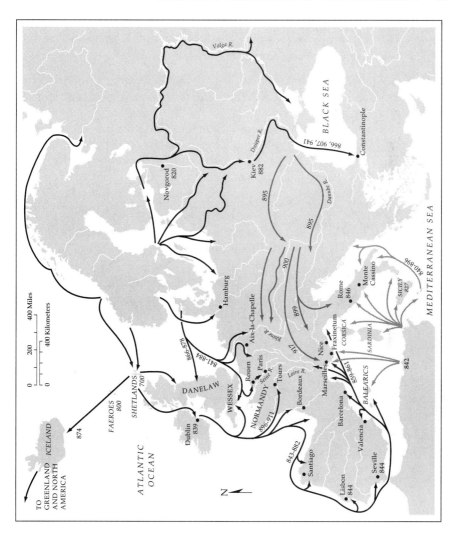

1. Indicate the homelands of the invading Vikings, Saracens, and Magyars; and show which arrows of invasions delineate routes taken by each of these three groups between the eighth and tenth centuries.
2. What does this map reveal about the political strength and vulnerability of Western Europe during these centuries?

PROBLEMS FOR ANALYSIS

I. *The New Community of Peoples*

1. Considering the numerous invasions of the Roman Empire by Celtic, Germanic, and Slavic tribes, was there a pattern to their conquests and settlements? Explain.
2. Despite many differences between Germans and Romans, the Germans assimilated into the culture of the Roman Empire. How do you explain this?
3. What legal, political, military, and cultural institutions did the Germans bring with them? Indicate any connections between these and later medieval institutions.

II. *The New Economy*

1. In what ways did Europeans make important technological and organizational changes in the economy of the Early Middle Ages?
2. What developments might help explain the decline of commerce and industry during the Early Middle Ages? What explanation makes the most sense to you?

III. *The Leadership of the Church*

1. How were the early Roman bishops able to develop themselves into powerful popes? What role did Gregory the Great play in this development?
2. Why was monasticism so important? What were the characteristics of monasticism? Why was the Benedictine rule so important?

IV. *The New Political Structures*

1. How were Carolingian leaders able to acquire power from their Merovingian predecessors and establish an extensive kingdom? Why was this kingdom short-lived?
2. Indicate the similarities and differences between the Anglo-Saxon and Frankish kingdoms. Consider the rise to power of unifying kings and the causes for their decline.

V. *Letters and Learning*

1. In what ways was Classical culture saved and transformed by the Church? Why was Classical culture so important to the Church?
2. What were the principal characteristics of the Carolingian Renaissance? Which of these were most important and why?

SPECULATIONS

1. Suppose you were a bishop of Rome during the Early Middle Ages. What do you think would be the best way to deal with the decline of the Roman Empire and the barbarian invasions? Why?
2. Do you think it is accurate to consider the Early Middle Ages a "dark age"? If our civilization fell, what would a corresponding "dark age" be like?

TRANSITIONS

In "The Empire and Christianity," the course and transformation of the Roman Empire were analyzed. By the fifth century, the Empire in the West fell and Christianity was established as the dominant religion in the Mediterranean area.

In "The Making of Western Europe," the beginnings of a new Western civilization are traced. It, like other new civilizations to the east and south that fell heir to the Classical tradition, differed most fundamentally from its Roman predecessor by being predominantly peasant and dominated by beliefs in an afterlife and hope of personal salvation. In Western Europe peoples combined "barbarian" and Classical inheritances to form distinctive cultures during the Early Middle Ages. Despite a long period of invasions and migrations, these peoples, supported by the settled peasant family and Roman Catholic beliefs, created a relatively poor, rural, and unstable civilization, which became the basis for Western civilization.

In "The Early Medieval East," the three civilizations of Byzantine, Kiev, and Islam will be examined and compared with those of Western Europe during the Early Middle Ages.

SEVEN
THE EARLY MEDIEVAL EAST

MAIN THEMES

1. The Eastern Roman Empire survived and evolved into the long-lasting Byzantine Empire.
2. The first East Slavic civilization was organized around the Principality of Kiev, a sophisticated but relatively short-lived state.
3. In the seventh century Islam rapidly expanded, conquering and converting vast areas and developing an advanced urban civilization.

OUTLINE AND SUMMARY

I. *The Byzantine Empire*

The Roman Empire did not fall in the East until 1453.

1. *The Early Byzantine Period*

Byzantine history begins in 324, when Constantine transferred his capital to Byzantium (Constantinople) for military purposes. Soon this city, located at the intersection of commercial routes, became a flourishing Christian center.

    a. *Justinian the Great:* Justinian (527–565) was the most successful of the early emperors who struggled to recover the full empire. From information supplied by Procopius we know much of Justinian, his ambitions, his influential wife Theodora, and his capable advisers. After nearly losing power during a rebellion, Justinian turned to ambitious projects. He partially succeeded in restoring western areas to the empire by defeating the Vandals in North Africa, the Ostrogoths in Italy, and the Visigoths in southern Spain. He organized and codified Roman law in the *Corpus Iuris Civilis,* which would form the basis for most Western legal systems. He initiated an extensive rebuilding of his capital, creating many new churches (church of Hagia Sophia), palaces, and public works. Toward the end of his reign Byzantium was faced by war in the east and the west and had to go on the defensive. Justinian's successors were unable to hold on to most of his territorial acquisitions.

2. The Middle Byzantine Period

The Emperor Heraclius (610–641) gave Byzantium its Eastern orientation. He succeeded against the aggressive Persians and followed a policy of granting land to soldiers and encouraging them to settle there (system of themes), making them more effective workers and fighters. After 632 Muslims overran most of the empire and held it until Leo III (717–741) began a reconquest of Asia Minor. In the following centuries warrior emperors recovered areas in the East, the Balkan Peninsula, southern Italy, and the Caucasus. A temporary policy forbidding the veneration of images (iconoclasm) further split Western and Eastern Churches.

3. Byzantine Civilization

Byzantines expanded Hellenistic ideas of natural law into a religious belief in one empire and one faith. The empire thus united its many peoples religiously and politically. The emperor was a holy figure who held political and religious authority (caesaropapism), though the extent of his religious authority has been questioned, since he was not a priest.

a. *The Two Churches:* A comparison of the Eastern and Western Churches clarifies other contrasts between the two peoples. The Eastern Church developed and functioned under secular supervision, while the Western Church freed itself from secular control and often assumed secular powers itself. Both considered themselves universal and orthodox. The two Churches maintained nearly identical beliefs, with some differences concerning the nature of the Holy Spirit, the existence of purgatory, and the legitimacy of divorce. The Eastern Church tolerated the use of vernacular languages, leading to an earlier development of vernacular literature than in the West, which tolerated only Latin. The Eastern Church was much more decentralized and dependent upon secular authority; in turn, the state in the East made use of the great wealth and spiritual power of the Church. The lack of friction between Church and state encouraged submissiveness and withdrawal by the Eastern Church in deference to the state.

b. *Byzantine Society:* Urban life survived, and some of the greatest cities of the age (Trebizond, Constantinople) were located within the empire. Rural society was largely made up of free peasants who participated in a highly developed village government. Economically, the empire was relatively wealthy, thanks to its commerce and its productive guilds (making mostly luxury items). The state retained some monopolies, particularly over silk products. Government was centralized under the emperor and his elaborate civil service. The government remained much more efficient and professional than in the West, with such refinements as an effective fiscal system, a state post, a secret police, and a corps of trained diplomats. Preference for eunuchs in governmental service, especially in palace administration, led to a gradual seclusion of women within the household.

c. *Byzantine Culture:* Byzantine wealth supported a tradition of learning among the clergy and some laypeople. Scholars used Greek and preserved almost all we know of Classical Greek literature. Architects created impressive structures, the greatest of all being the Hagia Sophia. Although marred by the iconoclastic movement, the Byzantines excelled in creating colorful but relatively static mosaics.

4. Decline of the Empire

As the system of themes began to weaken in the tenth century, the free peasants were transformed into serfs. Power slipped from the central government into the hands of strong local landlords. With a weakened navy, emperors became more dependent on Venetian naval power.

   a.   *The Seljuks:* In the eleventh century most of Asia Minor was conquered by the Seljuk Turks, ending the Byzantine Empire as a great power in the East.

   b.   *Schism with the West:* In 1054 rivalry, disputes, and snobbery led to a formal schism between the Eastern and Western churches.

5. The Western Debt to Byzantine Civilization

The Byzantine Empire helped protect the West from invasions, provided an example of advanced civilized life when the West was at a low point, and preserved Classical Greek literature.

II. The Principality of Kiev

The East Slavs (the Rus) founded a civilization based on the values of Eastern Christianity during the Early Middle Ages.

1. The Foundations of Kievan Rus

Between the sixth and ninth centuries the East Slavs expanded and founded Kiev and Novgorod. According to the *Primary Chronicle,* in the ninth century East Slavs, under the leadership of Vikings, became unified in the territory between Novgorod and Kiev. Oleg (873?–913) and his successors founded the Rus state. In 989 Vladimir converted to Eastern Christianity and brought the East Slavs into the Eastern cultural world.

   a.   *Yaroslav the Wise:* Under Yaroslav (1015–1054), the Principality of Kiev reached its height. He expanded his territorial control, gained independence for the Rus Church, codified laws, built cathedrals, promoted learning, and developed contacts with the West.

2. Kievan Civilization

Kievan economy was primarily agricultural, but there was considerable trade with surrounding peoples and civilizations, particularly with the Byzantines. Peasants were generally free, though there were some serfs and slaves. Kiev was considered one of the great cities of the age. Kievan government was a balance of monarchical, aristocratic, and popular elements, the prince relying on advice from his nobles (boyars) and his assemblies. Popular courts handled legal matters. Eastern Christianity brought the influence of Byzantine education, literature (*Primary Chronicle, Song of Igor's Campaign*), art (icons), and architecture (the onion domes). The East Slavs came to view their country as Holy Rus, alone against a sea of pagan barbarians.

3. Decline of the Principality

Political quarrels weakened Kiev internally. Steppe nomads cut off contract with the Black Sea, and thus trade with the Byzantine Empire. By the twelfth century, Kiev had been sacked and the center of Rus life moved north around Moscow.

III. Islam

Followers of Muhammad exploded out of Mecca in the seventh century, conquering and partially converting territories larger than the Roman Empire.

1. The Arabs

The Arabs, molded by the harsh environment of the Arabian peninsula, were proud animal herders and warriors. Their land was a focus of territorial and religious rivalry when Muhammad arrived.

2. Muhammad

Muhammad rose from humble origins in Mecca. He experienced revelations after 610, and in 622 he fled from Mecca to Yathrib (Medina), where he became a political leader. He combined his concern for law, administration, and government with religious conversion: Through enthusiastic proselytizing and war, his teachings spread rapidly.

3. The Religion of Islam

Muhammad believed that he received the prophecies of Allah ("the God") from the angel Gabriel. He passed them on to his followers, who collected them in the Koran. The Muslim religion emphasizes the power and concern of Allah; followers are to submit to the will of Allah and follow an ethically and legally upright life. Muslims have no clergy; there is but one sacred community of Allah, created by Allah through Muhammad and the Koran.

   a. *Expansion of Islam:*   Islam had great appeal to Arabs. It was relatively simple; it combined familiar features of Christianity, Judaism, paganism, and perhaps Zoroastrianism; and it depended on the Arabic language. The Arabs' policy of encouraging conquest while tolerating Christians and Jews aided in the rapid spread of the religion and of Islamic rule. There was a sudden expansion under the first four caliphs (632–661) and continued expansion under the Umayyads. Islam's extension into Europe was finally halted by Charles Martel at Tours in 732.

b. *The Schism:* In the eighth and ninth centuries internal religious and political rivalries combined with overexpansion to break Islam apart into independent caliphates.

4. Islamic Civilization

Islamic civilization reached its peak in the ninth and tenth centuries. Its expanse made it a varied civilization, though its common religion and language brought some unity. Commerce was particularly important, the merchant being a highly esteemed figure. A cosmopolitan urban life in the great cities (Baghdad, Cairo, Córdoba, Damascus) flourished. Spain and Baghdad became strong centers of this civilization. Males dominated women to an unusual degree, particularly among the upper classes. The caliph was, in theory, the supreme religious and civil authority; but in practice, he was primarily a military chief and a judge. Islamic scholars preserved works of the Greeks and added their own contributions in astronomy, astrology, mathematics, medicine, and optics. Their development of the zero, Arabic numerals, and algebra was particularly important. Scholars, such as Averroës, wrote philosophical and theological treatises that exerted a profound influence on both Christian and Islamic philosophy.

5. Challenges to Medieval Islamic Civilization

During the eleventh century, Christians went on the offensive in the West and the Mediterranean, breaking Islamic control and commerce in various areas. Meanwhile, in the East, Turks gained supremacy. Internally, commerce declined, and an aristocracy of rural warriors grew, bringing a new rigidity into society.

6. The Western Debt to Islamic Civilization

The West borrowed many specific accomplishments of Islam, such as their cultivation of new crops, their system of numbers, and their scholarship; but the West and Islam developed along separate paths.

GUIDE TO DOCUMENTS

From the Institutes of Justinian

1. What are the distinctions between the civil law of Rome and the law of all nations, and why might these distinctions be important?
2. In what ways might these principles of jurisprudence relate to assumptions we hold today about law and justice?

Literacy Comes to Rus

1. How did the Slaves perceive Byzantium?
2. In what ways might the introduction of Christianity into Slavic areas carry with it the cultures and civilizations of Byzantium and the West?

The Koran on Christians and Jews

1. How might this excerpt help explain the appeal of Islam?
2. How might this view of possible connections between Islam and Christians differ from views held by Christians about possible connections between Christians and Islam?

SIGNIFICANT INDIVIDUALS

Political Leaders

Justinian (527–565), Byzantine emperor.

Heraclius (610–641), Byzantine emperor.

Oleg (873?–913), founder, Rus state.

Theodora (527–548), Byzantine empress.

Vladimir (980–1015), Rus ruler.

Yaroslav (1015–1054), Rus ruler.

Cultural Leaders

Procopius (6th century), Byzantine historian.

Al-Mumun (813–833), caliph and patron of philosophy.

ibn-Rushd (Averroës) (1126?–1198), Islamic philosopher.

Religious Leaders

Muhammad (570–632), founder of Islam.

CHRONOLOGICAL DIAGRAM

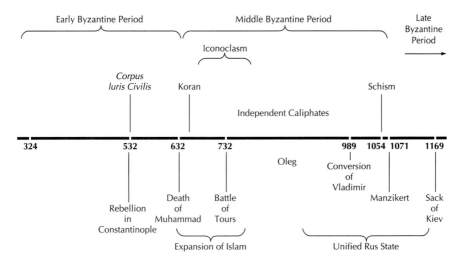

IDENTIFICATION

Constantinople
Hagia Sophia
iconoclasm
"caesaropapism"
Byzantine mosaics
Seljuk Turks
East Slavs

rota system
Koran
Umayyad caliphs
independent caliphates
Battle of Tours
Mecca
zero

MAP EXERCISES

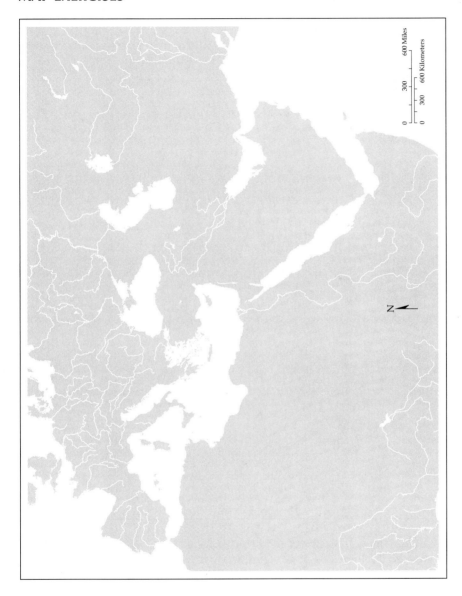

1. Indicate the areas of Islamic, Byzantine, and East Slavic control during the
   tenth and eleventh centuries.

1. Outline the boundaries of the Principality of Kiev in the eleventh century. Indicate the locations of Novgorod, Moscow, and the city of Kiev.

PROBLEMS FOR ANALYSIS

I. *The Byzantine Empire*

1. Justinian was both successful and unsuccessful in carrying out his ambitious plans. Compare his accomplishments with his ambitions. Do you think he would be considered a Roman or a Byzantine emperor? Why?
2. Compare the Eastern and the Western Churches. How did their connections to secular authority differ?
3. Develop a well-supported argument that the Byzantine Empire—in its cities, its economy, its government, and its culture—became the center of the civilized world around the Mediterranean after the fall of Rome.
4. Explain the decline of the Byzantine Empire.

II. *The Principality of Kiev*

1. Should the Principality of Kiev be considered one of the most advanced civilizations of its time? Why?
2. Should the Principality of Kiev be thought of as the foundation of modern Russia? Why?

III. *Islam*

1. How do you explain the extremely rapid spread of Islam in the seventh century? Was it mainly due to the nature of the religion? What role did the characteristics and environment of the Arabs play in this? Was it simply a function of conquest?
2. Compare the cosmopolitan Islamic civilization with the civilization of Western Europe during the Early Middle Ages. How did they differ politically and culturally?
3. In some ways Islam significantly influenced the West, yet some historians argue that the two civilizations were fundamentally separate. Do you agree? Why?

SPECULATIONS

1. If you were transported back in time as the chief adviser to Justinian, what would you recommend? Why?
2. Suppose the Western Roman Empire survived in a shrunken form—confined to Italy and areas bordering the Mediterranean in France, Spain, and northwestern Africa. Speculate on how this might have changed the course of European and Islamic history.

TRANSITIONS

In "The Making of Western Europe," the development of a new civilization in the West from a mixture of "barbarian" and Roman peoples during the Early Middle Ages was examined.

In "The Early Medieval East," the focus is shifted to three Eastern civilizations that arose during this same period: Byzantine, Kiev, and Islam. Byzantium developed directly from the old Roman Empire, evolving into a distinct civilization but retaining a strong continuity with the past. Kiev was heavily influenced by contact with Byzantium. Islam influenced the West, but remained fundamentally unique and apart. These civilizations enjoyed a clear superiority over those in Western Europe, thanks to the preservation of Roman institutions; the Hellenistic, Semitic, and Persian cultural heritages; the survival of cities; and the creation of an authentic urban life. Western Europe would benefit from the security against invasions from Asia, enlarged access to the Classical heritage, and new learnings offered by the presence of these Eastern civilizations.

In "Two Centuries of Creativity," we will return to the West, where striking changes led to a more firmly established civilization after the year 1000.

EIGHT
TWO CENTURIES OF
CREATIVITY

MAIN THEMES

1. After 1000, the European population expanded, commerce increased, and cities grew.
2. European society stabilized through the spread of feudal institutions and the rule of more effective kings.
3. The clergy and papacy gained in strength and influence through reform of the Church.
4. The period was one of the high cultural creativity marked by increased schooling, new interest in the humanities, and greater construction of Romanesque churches.

OUTLINE AND SUMMARY

I. Economic and Social Changes

After 1000, Europe entered a new period of change and growth.

1. The Beginnings of Expansion

Europeans began spreading out from impacted settlements after the year 1000. They cleared land, established new villages, and extended frontiers. Historians are not certain why this occurred, but factors such as fewer invasions, improved climate, and encouragement from landlords were probably involved. A sustained population growth resulted.

    a. *Frontiers:* Within Western Europe, peasants leveled forests and drained marshes. Other pioneers pushed outside frontiers to the east and north. Christian Europeans began reconquering Spain, Italy, and the western Mediterranean.

2. Social Changes

Expansion and economic revival led to improved conditions for peasants. Increasingly, they were able to free themselves from serfdom until it nearly disappeared throughout Western Europe by the thirteenth century. Landlords became less tied to their land, relying on rents, which freed them to travel and share in courtly society.

a. *Peasant Life:* Life for peasants, and particularly women, remained relatively harsh. Local commerce and cottage industries grew in importance. Rural churches grew as did the importance of the literate local priest.

b. *The Rise of the Nobility:* The appearance of a hereditary nobility reflected the growth in importance of patrilineage among elite families. The eldest son became the sole heir among elite families; daughters were provided with dowries. Excluded sons often drifted as knights-errant.

3. The Revival of Commerce

There was a major rebirth of long-distance trade during the Central Middle Ages. In the Mediterranean, Venice, Pisa, and Genoa led in developing trade between Europe, North Africa, and the East. Trade in the north grew between major ports around the Baltic. Between the two zones, overland trade developed, particularly at the great fairs of Champagne in France.

4. The Rebirth of Urban Life

Towns grew, though still at a relatively slow pace. They expanded from simple administrative centers and fortified enclosures to permanent centers of commerce and, later, industry (especially woolen cloth). Urban populations, especially the wealthy in northern Italy and Flanders, organized into communes and gained considerable liberties from their bishops or lords. Social movement between urban aristocrats (patricians), small merchants (now forming into guilds), and others was relatively fluid; talent was rewarded in this dynamic environment. Increased demand for skill in calculations and literacy characterized the developing culture of medieval towns.

II. Feudalism and the Search for Political Order

To differing degrees, European communities sought political stability through the institutions of the feudal system.

1. Feudal Institutions

Feudalism is an extraordinarily difficult term to define. To Marxist historians, it means an economic system based upon serfdom. To most non-Marxist scholars, it refers to the social and political institutions established by contract between a lord and his vassal. In a broader sense it refers to the society and government in which powerful men define their rights and obligations through individual contracts. Feudal practices developed spontaneously during the first feudal age (about 500–1050) and more self-consciously in the second (1050–1300).

a. *The Feudal Milieu:* Feudalism first grew in the region between the Loire and Rhine rivers, where alternatives for defense, such as familial (in Celtic and South Slavic areas) or communal (in northern Italy) associations, were lacking. It was then exported to other areas. Initially the bond was mainly ethical and emotional (quasi-familial), but later it became more juridical.

b. *Vassalage:* Vassalage refers to the bond between a lord and his vassal (inferior). It imposed upon both parties obligations of military support, financial aid, legal counsel, and moral support, the balance depending on the agreement and the relative power of the parties. Much of the lord's obligation was increasingly satisfied by a grant of land (fief). Over time, complications developed. Various courts claimed conflicting jurisdiction over vassals, and multiple vassalage created conflicting loyalties. Both developments signified a moral weakening of vassalage and an opportunity for monarchs to strengthen their authority.

c. *The Fief:* Theoretically, the fief granted by the lord to the vassal was conditional, temporary, and nonhereditary. In practice, however, the fief became inheritable and transferable upon the payment of a fee and the acquisition of the lord's permission. The spread of this form of land tenure between the ninth and twelfth centuries helped stabilize property and political relationships in Europe.

d. *Stages of Feudal Development:* In the ninth and tenth centuries, Carolingian administration disintegrated into local hands, especially holders of castles (castellans). Lords and vassals could tax, judge, and punish their dependents. During the next two centuries these fortresses proliferated. After 1050 a slow process of feudal centralization began under counts, dukes, and some kings. Royal prerogatives slowly diminished private justice.

2. Norman and Angevin England

England offers the best example of feudal concepts in the service of princes.

a. *The Norman Conquest:* The energetic Duke William of Normandy (1027–1087) conquered the English army at the Battle of Hastings in 1066. He decisively added to changes already taking place, making his vassals more directly tied to the monarchy and spreading feudal institutions, such as the great council, from the continent. Feudal obligations were clarified by a comprehensive survey of English lands (the *Domesday Book*).

b. *Angevin Kingship:* Henry II, a descendant of William, was the first of the "Angevin" kings, and one of England's best. Through inheritances and his marriage to Eleanor of Aquitaine, he ruled over England and western France. He developed a more effective system of justice, relying on authoritative itinerant judges who impounded "good men" of a locale to investigate crime and settle civil disputes. Decisions became precedents for similar cases, and over time, a body of "common" law was established that would serve the English-speaking world.

c. *Thomas Becket:* Henry II and the archbishop of Canterbury, Thomas Becket, struggled over the authority of Church (canonical) courts. The murder of Thomas led to the defeat of Henry on this issue.

3. Capetian France

After the age of Charlemagne, central government almost disappeared in France. After 1050 French kings followed a policy of developing lord-vassal relations with rulers of important principalities (such as Normandy, Flanders, and Champagne), slowly building some authority.

   a. *The Capetians:* Hugh Capet was elected king in 987, and his descendants held the throne until 1792. Initially the French kings held only limited, but strategically located, territory around Paris. They consolidated their power and eventually, under Louis VI (1108–1137) and Philip II, extended royal territories north and south.

   b. *Administration:* By improving financial and judicial administration, respecting the governments of fiefs, and insisting on the loyal service of great dukes and counts, French kings built upon feudal practices to strengthen central authority and political order.

4. The German Empire

In the tenth and eleventh centuries German political power became concentrated in comparatively large blocks under dukes who, facing the eastern frontiers, considered themselves champions of the Christian faith.

   a. *Otto I, the Great:* Otto I (936–973) was the first of the Saxon kings and restorer of the German Empire. He enjoyed military successes and promoted German missionaries in the East. He invaded Italy and was crowned Roman emperor by Pope John XII. This newly acquired prestige, combined with access to Church resources (control of office and lands), increased his power in German and Italian lands.

   b. *Frederick I, Barbarossa:* Under the powerful Frederick I of Hohenstaufen (1152–1190) the German Empire acquired a lasting foundation and would later be known as the Holy Roman Empire. Frederick was somewhat successful in consolidating his power in Germany, using his feudal powers to subdue the duke of Saxony. He attempted to establish effective control as heir to the Caesars, but a coalition of Italian towns (the Lombard League), supported by the papacy, defeated him at Legnano in 1176. This was the first time an army of townsmen had defeated an established army under noble leadership. His successors were unable to establish an effective government over his far-flung lands.

III. The Reform of the Western Church

In the eleventh and twelfth centuries the Church experienced fundamental and long-lasting transformations.

1. Moral Crisis

The Church suffered from a failure of its clergy to remain celibate, the sale of Church offices and services (simony), and lay dominion over Church offices and lands.

2. Early Attempts at Reform

Some bishops and German emperors attempted reforms, but with only limited success. The spread of Cluniac monasticism was more successful. The monastery of Cluny and its daughter houses throughout Europe were placed directly under the pope and Abbot of Cluny. Reformers started to turn to the long-degraded office of the pope for reform leadership.

3. Papal Reform

In the eleventh century reforming popes (Leo IX, Nicholas II) strengthened supervision of the Church, freed the papacy from military dependence on the German Empire, and succeeded in transferring the power to elect popes from the emperor to the College of Cardinals.

4. Gregory VII

Pope Gregory VII (1073–1085) made greater claims than ever for papal power, asserting authority over kings in at least spiritual matters.

a. *The Investiture Controversy:* Popes and Holy Roman Emperors struggled over the claims of laypeople to dispose of ecclesiastical offices and revenues by their own authority and in their own interests. The most famous confrontation came between Gregory VII and Emperor Henry IV in 1077. Gregory VII was symbolic victor over the penitent emperor at Canossa, but in reality, Henry came out ahead. In 1122 the controversy was settled by compromise, through the Concordat of Worms: Church appointments were to be made by the Church after consultation and compromise with the emperor.

b. *The Consolidation of Reform:* Long-lasting consequences flowed from Church reforms. The clergy was more separated than ever from the laity. Legal and administrative centralization gained in several ways. Above all, psychology of reform—humans have the power to face an evil world and improve it—fed into dynamic cultural attitudes that would characterize Westerners in centuries to come.

IV. The Cultural Revival

The period was marked by high cultural creativity.

1. The Rise of Universities

Between 1050 and 1200 the predecessor of universities, the cathedral (bishop's) school, assumed intellectual leadership in Europe. For both teachers and students, these schools were relatively fluid. A tradition of student life and wandering scholars developed. Slowly, discipline was imposed by the establishment of certification (the ancestor of modern academic degrees) and unification of masters and students into guilds. From these grew medieval universities, the first forming in Paris between 1200 and 1231. Italian schools followed a similar development but were built upon surviving professional schools, and there was a greater control by students over professors. From these institutions, organized for the pursuit of the preservation of learning, arose a class of people professionally committed to the life of thought.

2. Scholasticism

Most broadly, Scholasticism refers to medieval teaching in general. More specifically, it refers to medieval theology, especially the art of analyzing logical relationships among propositions in a dialogue or discourse (dialectic). St. Anselm was an early explorer of Scholastic thought (*Proslogium*). Abelard (*Sic et Non*) forcefully illustrated the power of Scholastic argumentation. Two other related trends developed: a growing interest in humanistic studies and a revival of Aristotelian philosophy. The reconciliation of Aristotelian reason and Christian beliefs became the central philosophical problem of the thirteenth century.

3. Vernacular Literature

There are three principal genres of vernacular literature that grew during the period. The heroic epic (*Song of Roland*) glorified masculine values. Troubadour lyric poetry, written for courts often dominated by females, celebrated women and love. The courtly romance (Crétien de Troyes) combined the two in tales of love and adventure.

4. Romanesque Art

The architectural and artistic style of the period is called Romanesque, a uniquely European combination of original and borrowed forms. It was most characterized by churches utilizing the groin vault to support stoned windowed roofs. Walls of these churches were decorated with antirealistic stone sculpture teeming with movement, reflecting the mystical spirit of the times. Religious need stimulated metalwork, glassmaking, and vestment weaving, as well as the development of polyphonic music (part-singing).

GUIDE TO DOCUMENTS

The Charter of Lorris

1. What inducements does the king offer to encourage the establishment and growth of towns?
2. What sorts of impediments to commerce in the medieval world are revealed by this document?

Louis VI Subdues a Violent Baron

1. What weapons were available to the Church to protect its interests?
2. What sorts of challenges to authority were presented to monarchs, and in what ways might monarchs meet those challenges, as revealed by this document?

Gregory VII's "Dictates of the Pope"

1. What powers does the pope claim for himself? By what methods might he back up those claims?
2. How does the pope justify his powers?

Abelard's "Sic et Non"

1. How are conflicts between authority and reason to be resolved according to Abelard?
2. In what ways might Abelard's Scholasticism be seen as encouraging analytical thought in general?

SIGNIFICANT INDIVIDUALS

Political Leaders

William of Normandy (1027–1087), king of England.

Harold Godwin (1066), king of England.

Henry II of Anjou (1154–1189), king of England.

Eleanor of Aquitaine (1137–1189), queen of France, England.

Hugh Capet (987–996), king of France.

Louis VI (1108–1137), king of France.

Philip II Augustus (1180–1223), king of France.

John (1199–1216), king of England.

Otto I (936–973), Saxon king, emperor.

Frederick I, Barbarossa (1152–1190), German emperor.

Religious Leaders

Thomas Becket (1118?–1170), archbishop of Canterbury.

Innocent III (1198–1216), pope.

Leo IX (1049–1054), reforming pope.

Gregory VII (1073–1085), reforming pope.

Cultural Figures

St. Anselm of Canterbury (1033–1109), Scholastic.

Peter Abelard (1079–1142), Scholastic.

Crétien de Troyes (12th century), French poet.

CHRONOLOGICAL DIAGRAM

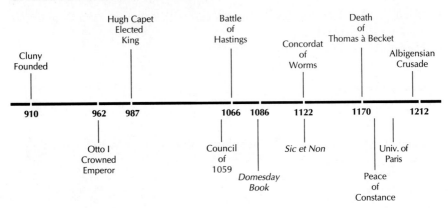

IDENTIFICATION

the *mansi*
Reconquista
"spices"
fairs of Champagne
commune
vassal
fief
private justice
castellans
Curia Regis (great council)

justices in eyre
the *bailli*
"Stem" duchies
simony
Cluniac monasticism
investiture controversy
Gregorian ideals
tithes
Scholasticism
Romanesque style

MAP EXERCISE

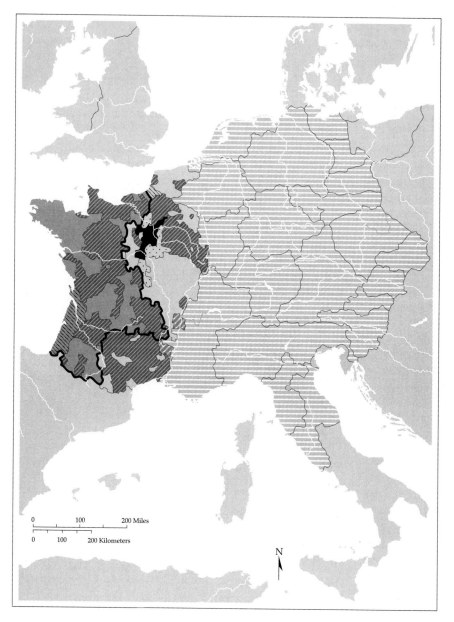

1. Label the main political units of Europe toward the end of the twelfth century.
2. What sorts of problems would France have to overcome before unifying the territory that would become modern France?

PROBLEMS FOR ANALYSIS

I. The Economic and Social Changes

1. Explain the causes and significance of the population changes that occurred during the eleventh and twelfth centuries.
2. In what ways was there a revival of commerce and social life during this period? Who benefited from this?

II. Feudalism and the Search for Political Order

1. Why was feudalism effective in promoting social order in Europe during the eleventh and twelfth centuries? What was the cement that held feudal relations together?
2. Compare the development of feudalism in any two countries. Explain the similarities and differences. Did feudalism function to strengthen or weaken the authority of the king?

III. The Reform of the Western Church.

1. What conditions created a need for reform within the Western Church?
2. What roles did popes and Cluniac monasticism play in the reform of the Church? What was so "reforming" about their activities?
3. What was the significance of the reform of the Western Church? Was it a movement that only affected the Church internally, or were there broader consequences? Explain.

IV. The Cultural Revival

1. Compare the universities and student life in the twelfth century with those of today. What was so important about the development of universities at this early date?
2. Did religious concerns completely dominate cultural life during the eleventh and twelfth centuries? Support your argument.

SPECULATIONS

1. Do you think there is something special about the year 1000? Explain.
2. What policies would you recommend to an eleventh-century king to maximize his power? Why?
3. Should we consider the Church special, or is it just an institution with problems like the government or any other institution? Can you support your view historically?

TRANSITIONS

In "The Early Medieval East," the development of three civilizations on the borders of the West was traced and compared with the new civilization in the West, which was just emerging during the Early Middle Ages.

In "Two Centuries of Creativity," focus is again on the West. The eleventh and twelfth centuries mark a new vigorous period of growth in Europe. So striking is the creativity at almost every level of life that some scholars believe this to be a medieval renaissance legitimately part of "traditional Europe," lasting until the eighteenth and nineteenth centuries.

In "The Summer of the Middle Ages," the civilization of the Middle Ages is at its peak and faces new problems.

NINE
THE SUMMER OF THE
MIDDLE AGES

MAIN THEMES

1. Agriculture, commerce, and industry expanded greatly in the thirteenth century.
2. In the various states of Europe, representative assemblies gained power, and constitutional stability improved.
3. The papacy greatly unified Europe spiritually, but it left a disturbing legacy of political and ecclesiastical problems.
4. In its Scholasticism, its Gothic style, and its culture, the thirteenth century was a period of intellectual synthesis.

OUTLINE SUMMARY

I. Economic Expansion

Commerce and agriculture were stimulated by demand and regional specialization; rents increased and wages fell.

1. The Cities

Commerce and industry developed dramatically. Medieval manufacturing took place mostly in the home. Merchants and manufacturers controlled the capital and provided the raw materials, while specialized artisans did the work (putting-out system). The manufacture of woolen cloth was the largest town industry, supporting many workers. The cloth was created in a series of steps (sorting, spinning, weaving, fulling, dyeing) performed by specialized workers.

2. The Guilds

Commercial classes promoted their interests by forming professional associations (guilds). By the twelfth century there were numerous specialized guilds of artisans and merchants. Guilds met regularly, set standards, provided for members' welfare, and undertook civic activities. They also developed the apprentice system, which provided for lay education and an ordered method for supplying skilled labor.

3. Business Institutions

Sophisticated commercial and banking institutions were developed. Since Christian ethics condemned interest payments on a loan (usury), alternatives, such as the bill of exchange, were developed. Capital was also recruited through temporary partnerships and business associations. In some Italian towns more permanent partnerships, or companies, were formed, some becoming extremely large. They performed important commercial and banking services, in some cases supporting kings and popes.

4. Medieval Views of Economic Life

Traditional Christian views were not positive toward property and wealth, accepting them as necessary evils. This changed somewhat in the thirteenth century. Thomas Aquinas gave property and wealth a basis in natural law and increased their dignity; merchants were not condemned as before. Yet there continued to be strong moral obligations to use property for the common good.

II. The States of Europe

During the thirteenth century governments gained constitutional stability and increasingly utilized representative assemblies.

1. England

The effective functioning of the English government—despite the almost perpetual absence of its warrior king, Richard the Lion-Hearted, and the humiliations of his successor John—is evidence for its fundamental strength.

   a. *Magna Carta:* The enraged barons, with the support of the Church, took up arms and forced John to grant the "Great Charter" of liberties (Magna Carta). In fact, it concerned mainly the elites and mostly specified legal feudal relationships. In it, the king promised not to disturb the customary liberties of the upper classes, to follow known legal procedures, and not to impose new taxes without consent from the upper classes (the realm). It was, however, a step toward constitutional government and a symbol of traditional balance between authority and liberty.

   b. *Legal Reforms:* Edward I (1272–1307) became one of England's greatest medieval kings. His most important accomplishment was the development and clarification of English law, especially real estate law.

   c. *Parliamentary Origins:* During the thirteenth century meetings of the traditional great council became more frequent. They were first called parliaments under Henry II. At some point Parliament was split into separate houses of Lords and Commons, with the Commons benefiting from the participation of the lower aristocracy and the eventual unwillingness of the upper clergy to serve in the House of Lords.

   d. *Representation:* Parliament gave advice to the king, supported his decisions, facilitated the collection of taxes, passed on new taxes, and served as England's highest court.

2. France

The thirteenth century was also an age of constitutional consolidation in France. Louis VIII helped expand French territories and solidify a monarchy based on inheritance.

a. *St. Louis:* The pious Louis IX was recognized as a saint during his lifetime. He acted strongly to improve justice, gain peace with his neighbors, and make war against the Muslims.

b. *Legal Reforms:* Louis' fairness and concern in legal matters gave great prestige to royal justice. The legal system was further strengthened by his codifying the laws (*Establishments of St. Louis*) and confirming the Parlement of Paris as France's highest court.

c. *Philip IV:* Philip warred unsuccessfully against the English and attempted to replenish his treasury by persecuting Jews, extorting money from foreign merchants, and arresting the wealthy Knights Templars within France. Philip struggled with Pope Boniface VIII over the right to tax the clergy. Philip was overly ambitious in his efforts to achieve an absolute monarchy, leaving a deeply disturbed France.

3. The Iberian Kingdoms

After the nearly complete success of the Christian *Reconquista* (1236), Spain was left in a disunified state. Even within the three major Christian kingdoms of Portugal, Castile, and Aragon, there were self-governing groups (Jews and Muslims) and towns (Barcelona, Valencia, Toledo, Seville). The military aristocracy was unusually independent, as were religious orders of knights. To bolster their power, Iberian kings used representative assemblies (Cortes) and systematized laws and customs. Having achieved stability, these kingdoms expanded into the Mediterranean as far as Athens.

4. The Holy Roman Empire

Facing geographic, cultural, and political obstructions to unity, the Holy Roman Empire disintegrated into a large number of small and virtually autonomous principalities.

a. *Frederick II Hohenstaufen:* The extraordinary Frederick II had renaissance interests in learning. His political and diplomatic style was similar to that of more modern rulers. He reinforced political fragmentation in Germany by granting virtual sovereignty to ecclesiastical princes and lay nobles within their own territories. He completed the constitutional reorganization of southern Italy and was the last emperor to take seriously the grand vision of a Christian empire.

III. The Church

The papacy came close to building a unified Christian commonwealth in Europe based on peace, faith, and obedience.

1. The Growth of Heresy

In the eleventh century heresies began appearing in Europe. The causes were complex: reaction to abuses in the Church, social dislocations caused by population growth, envy of Church wealth by nobles, discontent with Church and society by many women, and spiritual tension, leading many to try and break the monastic monopoly over the religious experience.

2. The Waldensians and the Albigensians

The Waldensians of southern France attacked moral laxness in the Church and followed a life of poverty. Though they were declared heretical in 1215, the Church never completely suppressed the movement. The Albigensians also attacked the Church and emphasized the struggle between good and evil. This became a strong movement but did not survive the Middle Ages.

3. The Suppression of Heresy

The new Dominican order attempted to reconvert the Albigensians. Pope Innocent III initiated a crusade against them in the early 1200s. In 1231 Pope Gregory IX instituted a special papal court to investigate and punish heresy (the papal Inquisition). A suspect—facing an assumption of guilt, secret denunciations, and torture—had little chance of proving innocence. The Inquisition eventually eroded the Church's prestige.

4. The Franciscans

The Franciscans, led by St. Francis of Assisi (1182?–1226), initiated spiritual regeneration in the thirteenth century. St. Francis combined piety, orthodoxy, and mystical insights. He quickly attracted followers, especially among laypeople in the growing towns, and his order grew to become the largest in the Church.

5. Papal Government

Pope Innocent III (1198–1216) best illustrates the aspirations and problems of the medieval Church. He tried to unify Christendom by eliminating heresy and bringing the Eastern Church under him, with mixed results. He struggled with European princes (John of England, Emperor Frederick II, Philip II of France, and others) for authority with similarly mixed results. He tried to clarify Christian discipline and beliefs.

6. The Papacy in the Thirteenth Century

In 1215 Innocent summoned the Lateran Council, which clarified such matters as the importance of the sacraments, transubstantiation, and priestly discipline. The papacy grew administratively and financially during the thirteenth century, but popes were becoming dependent on exploiting spiritual powers for financial profit.

a. *Boniface VIII:* Boniface VIII became entangled in struggles with secular rulers, leading to his temporary capture and, in 1309, to the election of the first in a series of French-supported popes in Avignon. The thirteenth-century papacy, though powerful at the top, weakened the ability of bishops to maintain discipline at the local level.

IV. The Summer of Medieval Culture

This was an age of intellectual synthesis.

1. The Medieval Synthesis

The principal intellectual effort of the time was to reconcile Aristotelian philosophy, based on the power of human reason, and Christian attitudes, based on the necessity of divine revelation and grace. This effort at synthesis can be seen in the Scholasticism of Thomas Aquinas, the Gothic cathedral, and the *Comedy* of Dante Alighieri.

2. Thomas Aquinas

St. Thomas Aquinas (1225?–1274) was the greatest Christian theologian since Augustine. In his *Summa Theologica* he argued that both faith and reason led to a single truth, and that while the universe was made up of individual objects, all objects were bound into a fundamental hierarchy under God. John Duns Scotus criticized Thomas, arguing that faith preceded reason and that God was an inherently necessary being.

3. The Gothic Cathedral

The Gothic style spread through Europe. The most stunning examples are the great urban churches. Gothic style is characterized by the broken arch, ribbed vaulting, flying buttresses, higher walls, large stained windows, and realistic statues.

a. *The Gothic Spirit:* The architectural style, the use of light, and the performance of the sacred liturgy with polyphonic music combined in these churches to convey a sense of order in a universe governed by a wise, loving, and present God.

4. Dante

Dante's *Comedy* best summarizes the culture of the age. His works were greatly influenced by two experiences: his early love for a young girl named Beatrice and his exile from Florence.

a. *The Comedy:* This poem tells how Dante, an aging man, is led through hell and purgatory by Virgil, who represents human reason, and to heaven by Beatrice, who represents supernatural revelation and grace. He thus dealt with his own life as well as the issues of his age by exploring the relation between optimistic, Classical rationalism and Christian faith in divine will.

GUIDE TO DOCUMENTS

Excerpts from "Magna Carta"

1. In what ways does this document reflect limitations on monarchical authority in England?
2. Which of these provisions might, in the long run, become the basis for common law rights for everyone?

The Techniques of the Inquisition

1. In what ways did the Church, through inquisitors such as Bernard Gui, attempt to combat heresy?
2. What, according to this document, were the essential beliefs of the Church that heretics might disagree with?

Unam Sanctam

1. What powers is the pope claiming in this document?
2. How does the pope justify these claims?
3. What would secular powers give up by accepting these claims?

SIGNIFICANT INDIVIDUALS

Political Leaders

Richard I, the Lion-Hearted (1189–1199), king of England.

Henry III (1216–1272), king of England.

Simon de Montfort (1208?–1265), English statesman and soldier.

Edward I (1272–1307), king of England.

St. Louis IX (1226–1270), king of France.

Philip IV, the Fair (1285–1314), king of France.

Frederick II Hohenstaufen (1194–1250), Holy Roman Emperor.

Religious Leaders

Peter Waldo (12th century), founder of Waldensians.

St. Francis of Assisi (1182?–1226), founder of the Franciscans.

Bernard Gui (12th century), inquisitor.

Innocent III (1198–1216), pope.

Boniface VIII (1294–1303), pope.

Clement V (1305–1314), pope at Avignon.

Cultural Figures

Thomas Aquinas (1225?–1274), Scholastic.
John Duns Scotus (1265?–1308), theologian.

Dante (1265–1321), Florentine poet.

CHRONOLOGICAL DIAGRAM

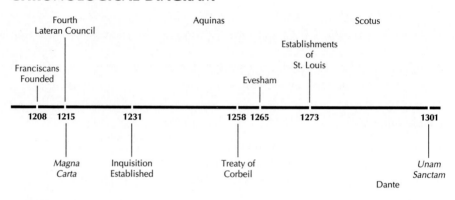

IDENTIFICATION

putting-out system
guilds
apprenticeship system
usury
bill of exchange
the companies
Parliament
Magna Carta

Parlement of Paris
Templars
Cortes
Waldensians
Albigensians
Inquisition
Summa Theologica
Gothic

MAP EXERCISE

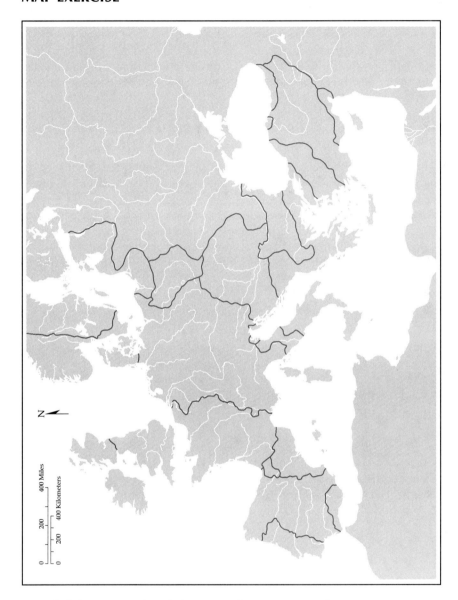

1. Label the main political divisions of Europe around 1250.

PROBLEMS FOR ANALYSIS

I. Economic Expansion

1. It can be argued that industry and commerce acquired many modern characteristics by the thirteenth century. Considering methods of manufacturing, the guilds, business institutions, and views toward economic life, do you agree? Why?

II. The States of Europe

1. The Magna Carta is sometimes thought of as a democratic document. In light of the political developments in England during the thirteenth century, do you agree? Why?
2. Compare constitutional consolidation in France with the disintegration of the Holy Roman Empire. How do you explain the differences?
3. Considering institutions such as Parliament, the Parlement of Paris, and the Cortes, should the thirteenth century be regarded politically as a period of representative assemblies? Why?

III. The Church

1. Does the growth of heresy, and its suppression, indicate that the Church was effectively unified during the thirteenth century? Why?
2. Compare the factors that evidenced the growing strength of the Church with those that evidenced future problems for the Church.

IV. The Summer of Medieval Culture

1. Compare the ideas of Aquinas and Duns Scotus. How does the analysis of Duns Scotus signify a change from the synthesis of Aquinas?
2. In what ways does Dante's *Comedy* summarize the culture of this age? Compare the *Comedy* of Dante with the *Summa Theologica* of Aquinas.

SPECULATIONS

1. If you could select any century between 400 and 1400 to live in, would you select the thirteenth century? What would the advantages and disadvantages be?
2. If you were a pope during the thirteenth century, what policies would you follow to promote the best interests of the Church?
3. Would you recommend to the thirteenth-century kings that they support representative assemblies or fight against them? Why?

TRANSITIONS

In "Two Centuries of Creativity," the quickening pace of development in the West was traced.

In "The Summer of the Middle Ages," the period between 1200 and 1348 is examined. During most of this time Europe enjoyed relative prosperity, peace, institutional stability, and intellectual synthesis. Yet overpopulation, misery among the poor, the specter of war, and intellectual and religious dissent also characterized the period. The relative successes of the thirteenth century would not survive the disasters and changes of the fourteenth and fifteenth centuries.

In "The Crusades and Eastern Europe," focus will shift to the East and to the growing connections between the two areas.

TEN
THE CRUSADES AND
EASTERN EUROPE

MAIN THEMES

1. The crusades, initiated for a variety of reasons, led to an expansion of Europeans into the East.
2. After the eleventh century, the Byzantine Empire declined until it was finally overwhelmed by the expanding Ottoman Empire in 1453.
3. Princes of Moscow succeeded in dealing with the powerful Mongols and founded the modern Russian state in the fifteenth century.

OUTLINE AND SUMMARY

I. The Crusades

In the eleventh century Western peoples launched a series of armed expeditions, known as the crusades, to the East in an effort to free the Holy Land from Islamic rule. While interpretations of the crusades differ, it is certain that they initiated a long-term expansion of the West beyond Europe.

1. Origins

Two circumstances led to the First Crusades: a conflict between increasing numbers of pilgrims traveling to Palestine and the Seljuk Turks, who controlled the area. An appeal by the declining Byzantium to Pope Urban II to help defend Constantinople against that same Islamic power was answered.

2. The Motives of the Crusaders

For participants, the crusades were acts of assertive religious devotion. But social and economic motivations were important. The crusades served as an outlet for a growing population, especially knights, who had few other opportunities for advancement in a stabilizing Europe. Moreover, many crusaders came from the violent fringes of society; the crusades provided them appropriate outlets.

3. The First Crusade

The First Crusade (1096–1099) was initiated by Pope Urban II's call to arms in 1095. There were two sorts of responses: one made up of peasants and the poor, who were roused to action by preachers (the Popular Crusade), and one that was more organized and led by various nobles. The first group was completely defeated by the Turks. The second was more successful, thanks to some help from Byzantium, daring military victories (Dorylaeum, Edessa, Antioch), and the Turkish inability to present a united front.

4. The Kingdom of Jerusalem

The crusaders established shaky but surprisingly long-lasting control over Near Eastern lands around Jerusalem, Tripoli, Antioch, and Edessa; and they applied feudal concepts and institutions there. They remained, however, a precarious foreign aristocracy in a hostile land.

5. The Later Crusades

Europeans conducted further crusades in the twelfth century, the last (1189–1192) constituting a great effort by Emperor Frederick Barbarossa, Philip II of France, and Richard I of England. Yet none of these enjoyed success, as the Turks slowly recaptured lands. The last Christian outpost on mainland Asia (Acre) was lost in 1291. By then the crusading spirit had long since diminished.

6. Results of the Crusades

In the long run, the crusades slowed the Turkish advance in the Mediterranean and Europe. There were other more indirect consequences. Castle construction was improved, military skills were copied on both sides, new taxing methods to support the crusades were developed, and the sale of indulgences to support the crusades was allowed.

7. Military-Religious Orders

Military-religious orders of knights (Templars, Hospitalers, and Teutonic Knights) were organized successfully to supply the East and to defend safe passage there. The Templars created a great banking institution, the Hospitalers became the long-lasting Knights of Malta, and the Teutonic Knights conquered extensive domains around the Baltic Sea.

8. Economy

The crusades increased the circulation of money and treasure, enlivened trade with the East, and created demands for Eastern commodities, which led Europeans to explore new ways to import Eastern spices and similar products.

9. Religion and Learning

With the exception of an increased geographic knowledge, the crusades had no great religious or intellectual consequences for either Christian or Islamic society.

II. *Byzantium and the Ascendancy of the Ottoman Empire*

After 1071 the Byzantine Empire's control was limited to Greece and the area around Constantinople.

1. *The Decline of Byzantium*

Crusaders stormed Constantinople in 1204 and divided the Byzantine Empire among themselves; Venetians gained the most. Elements of the old Byzantine Empire remained, but they were unable to prevent independent kingdoms of Bulgarians and Serbs from forming in the thirteenth and fourteenth centuries.

2. *The Fall of Constantinople*

Seljuk Turks, Mongols, and Ottoman Turks, in turn, dominated the Middle East between the eleventh and fourteenth centuries. Constantinople finally fell to the Ottomans in 1453. The fall shocked the Christian world and stimulated efforts to find new trade routes to the East. It also symbolizes, for many historians, the end of the Middle Ages.

3. *Expansion of the Ottoman Empire*

In the fifteenth century the Ottomans entered upon a century of expansion. Mehmet II made the Ottomans a major land and sea power, especially in southeastern Europe. Other rulers led conquests in Arab lands in the early sixteenth century. Suleiman II (1520–1566) led the empire to its height of power, extending borders in the west to the gates of Vienna and Algeria, and in the east to Arabia and Persia. He became a diplomatic ally of France against Charles V, the Holy Roman Emperor, leading to commercial ties with France.

4. *Ottoman Institutions*

Ottomans took advantage of their geographic position, internal political and religious feuds among Christians, and strong military traditions to create their empire. They organized conquered territories well; followed tolerant policies that allowed religious, social, economic, and cultural practices of conquered peoples to continue; and developed effective military and administrative institutions. Ottoman sultans ruled through a council of advisers (the divan) presided over by an administrative officer (the grand vizier). Religious affairs were administered by a class of judges. The army was made up of unpaid holders of fiefs granted by the sultan in exchange for military service, and of paid soldiers, who were technically considered slaves. Janissaries, an elite corps of professional soldiers, became the backbone of Ottoman victories. Local government was usually left to self-governing communities of Christians and Jews and to the holders of fiefs. A new system of recruitment for palace administration and the corps of Janissaries, based on the early selection of boys for intense training, was developed in the fifteenth century and became a fundamental institution of the empire.

5. The Sultan

The sultan retained supreme civil, military, and religious authority. Power was transferred to successors by the law of fratricide, which provided that a designated son would take office and his brothers would be put to death.

6. The Limits of Ottoman Power

After Suleiman the Magnificent, there were no further expansions. Newly developing trade routes decreased the commercial importance of the Ottoman Empire, and succeeding sultans lacked the dynamism of earlier rulers. The Ottomans were slowly left behind by the advancing energetic Europeans.

III. The Birth of Modern Russia

Pressured by raiding nomads in the south and east, the Rus colonized and built new civilizations in the forests to the north and west.

1. The Mongols

Between the thirteenth and fifteenth centuries, a division of the Mongol Empire (the Golden Horde) was the supreme power over most of Russia. Mongols exacted recognition (*yarlik*) and tribute from the East Slavs, allowing them to maintain their local control, their language, and their culture. Mongol pressure forced the Rus north and west into three areas: Galicia, Novgorod, and Russian Mesopotamia (between the upper Volga and the Oka rivers). The latter area became the nucleus of a new Russian state. From the twelfth to the fifteenth centuries there was no central government; local princes held the power. The economy was almost completely agricultural, and society was made up primarily of free peasants. Culturally, Russia's wooden churches and icon painting (Andrei Rublev) stand out.

2. The Rise of Moscow

A central location and the talent of its early princes made Moscow the leader of Russia. Its princes added territory through war, marriage, and purchase, and made Moscow a symbol of national unity in the face of Mongols and Western Christians. Ivan I (1328–1341) added territories, obtained a privileged position with the Mongols, and courted the Russian Church. Dimitri successfully led Russians to their first victory over the Mongols in 1380. Ivan the Great (1462–1505) and his successor Basil II completed the process of gathering Russian land, freeing Russia from the power of the Golden Horde, and founding modern Russia.

3. Institutional and Social Change

Ivan III founded the modern Russian state by depicting himself as the successor of Byzantine emperors, promulgating a new code of laws (*Sudebnik*), creating a new class of serving gentry, and unifying Russia to face the outside world. He passed on to his successors a centralized, autocratic government.

GUIDE TO DOCUMENTS

Arabic and Frankish Medicine

1. What does this reveal about the comparative state of medical practices among Muslims and Franks?
2. What does this reveal about the possibilities and barriers to cross-cultural learning during this period?

The Sultan Mehmet II

1. What impression might English readers get of Mehmet II after reading this description by Richard Knolles?
2. What does this reveal about the mixture of Mediterranean cultures during the fifteenth century?

The Janissaries

1. What, according to this observer, is the basis for the strength of the Janissaries?
2. How does Busbecq compare the Ottoman and Christian soldiers?

The Birth of Christianity in Russia

1. What lesson is a thirteenth-century reader of this document supposed to draw from this account?
2. What, according to this account, was the appeal of the Greek church?

SIGNIFICANT INDIVIDUALS

Political Leaders

Baldwin (1058–1118), crusader.
Constantine XIII (1448–1453), last Byzantine emperor.
Mehmet II, the Conqueror (1451–1481), Ottoman sultan.
Osman (1288–1326), founder of the Ottoman dynasty.
Suleiman II, the Magnificent (1520–1566), Ottoman sultan.

Genghis Khan (1206–1227), khan of Mongols.
Ivan I (1328–1341), Muscovite prince.
Ivan III, the Great (1462–1505), tsar of Russia.
Basil III (1505–1533), tsar of Russia.

Cultural Figure

Andrei Rublev (1370?–1430?),
  Russian religious painter.

CHRONOLOGICAL DIAGRAM

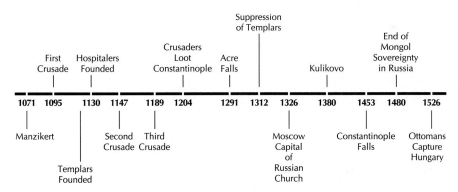

IDENTIFICATION

Saladin tithe	vizier
Hospitalers	Janissaries
Teutonic Knights	law of fratricide
yarlik	Russian Mesopotamia
Golden Horde	*Sudebnik*

MAP EXERCISES

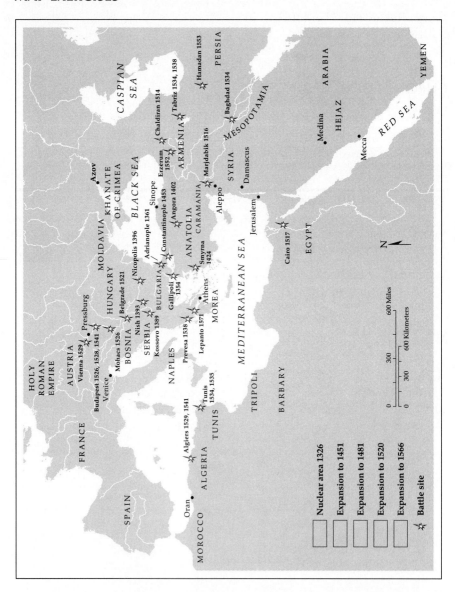

1. Indicate the expansion of the Ottoman Empire between 1300 and 1566.
2. Indicate the location of the Crusader kingdoms.

1. Show those areas applying pressure to the East Slavs in the Principality of Kiev.
2. Show the movement of the East Slavs as the Principality of Kiev collapsed.

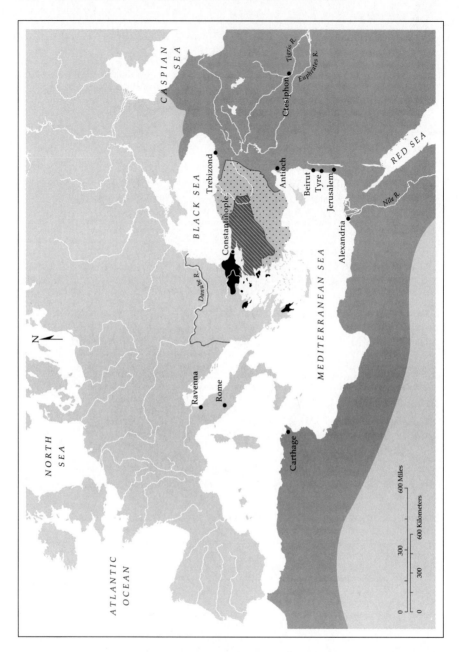

1. Label those areas controlled by the Mongols, Turks, Islam, and Byzantium around 1350.

PROBLEMS FOR ANALYSIS

I. The Crusades

1. What circumstances led to the First Crusades? What balance of religious, economic, and social motives do you think led people to participate in these crusades?
2. Considering the effort involved and the result of the crusades, were they a success or a failure? Why?
3. What were the most important consequences of the crusades? Is it fair to argue that the crusades proved to be of greater economic than religious significance for Europe? Why?

II. Byzantium and the Ascendancy of the Ottoman Empire

1. In what ways did the decline of Byzantium lead to important changes in the Mediterranean and the West?
2. How did the various Ottoman institutions contribute to the successful rise and expansion of this powerful empire? What role did the sultan and the Janissaries play?

III. The Birth of Modern Russia

1. Why did Moscow become the center of the Russian state? What role did the relations between the Mongols and the prince of Moscow play in this?
2. On what basis should Ivan III be considered the founder of the modern Russian state? What policies did he pursue to this end?

SPECULATIONS

1. At times, it appeared that either the Mongols or the Turks might sweep through Europe. Suppose that happened. How do you think it might have changed the development of Europe?
2. Considering your knowledge of the crusades, what sort of cause might lead you to join a "crusade"? What would your motives be?
3. Do you think Pope Urban II was justified in calling for the First Crusade?

TRANSITIONS

In "The Summer of the Middle Ages," the civilization of the Middle Ages in the West at its peak was examined, a civilization that benefited from two previous centuries of creative development.

In "The Crusades and Eastern Europe," focus is shifted eastward. After 1000 the Byzantine, Arab, and Kievan civilizations were all in decline. The Seljuks and then the Ottomans gained as the Byzantine and Arab states weakened, and a new Russia state centered at Moscow grew. Religious, commercial, and military contacts between the East and West grew, above all through the crusades and commercial expansion of Western Europe.

In "The West in Transition: Economy and Institutions," we will see a shift to more troubled times in the West during the fourteenth and fifteenth centuries.

SECTION SUMMARY
THE MIDDLE AGES AND
THE MEDIEVAL EAST
500–1300
CHAPTERS 6–10

CHRONOLOGICAL DIAGRAM

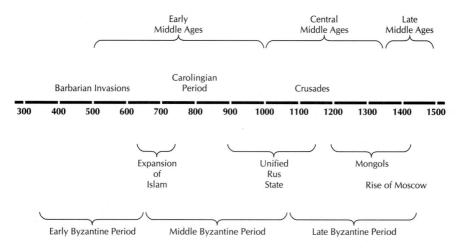

MAP EXERCISES

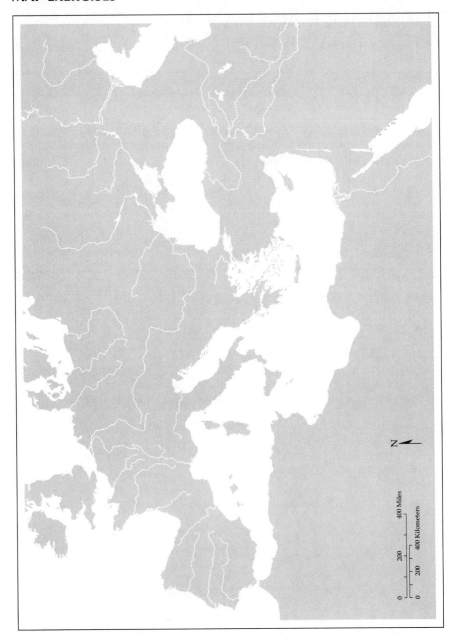

1. Indicate the following:
   a. Areas controlled by the Byzantine Empire during the early period, the middle period, and the late period. Indicate the approximate dates for each.
   b. Areas controlled by Islam at its maximum point of westward expansion. Indicate the approximate date.
   c. Areas controlled by Charlemagne. Indicate the approximate date.

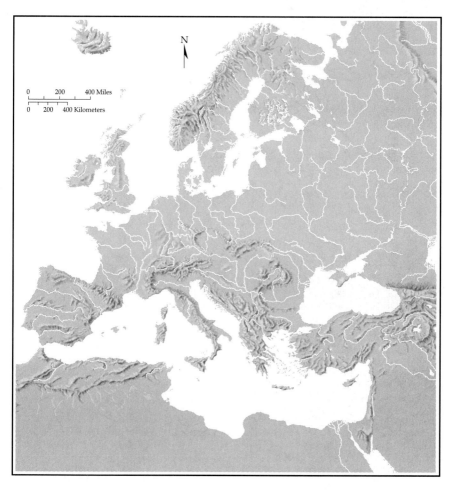

1. Indicate the crusader kingdoms and their approximate dates.
2. Indicate the political division of Europe around 1250.
3. Indicate the areas controlled by the Ottoman Turks around 1550.

1. Indicate the areas controlled by the early Rus state (Kiev). Indicate the approximate date.
2. Indicate approximate areas controlled by the Mongols around 1300.
3. Indicate the Russian state around 1500.

BOX CHARTS

Reproduce the Box Charts in a larger format in your notebook or on separate sheets of paper.

Chart 1

	Political Institutions and Developments	Economic System and Characteristics	Social System and Characteristics	Religious System and Characteristics	Cultural Values and Productions
Byzantium to ca. 1000					
Rus to ca. 1200					
Islam to ca. 1100					
Europe to ca. 1000					

Chart 2

Europe: Characteristics, Developments, Turning Points

	1000 ———————→ 1300	Regional Differences
Political Institutions and Developments		
Economic System and Characteristics		
Social System and Characteristics		
Religious System and Characteristics		
Cultural Values and Productions		

Chart 3

	Europe 1300 ⟶ 1559	Turning Points	Problems
Political Institutions and Developments			
Economic System and Characteristics			
Social System and Characteristics			
Religious System and Characteristics			
Cultural Values and Productions			

ELEVEN
THE WEST IN TRANSITION:
ECONOMY AND INSTITUTIONS

MAIN THEMES

1. Europeans suffered economic dislocations and demographic disasters in the fourteenth and fifteenth centuries.
2. Europe suffered from depressions in trade and industry, but then recovered.
3. Economic, psychological, and social factors led the lower classes in rural and urban areas to revolt, adding to the upheaval of the period.
4. Wars, weakening central authority, and questions about royal succession reflected the considerable political instability of the period.
5. The papacy suffered a major schism and growing unpopularity, which seriously weakened its authority.

OUTLINE AND SUMMARY

I. *Population Disaster and Agricultural Change*

In the fourteenth and fifteenth centuries, plagues and famines struck Europe with varying effects.

1. *Demographic Catastrophe*

Europe suffered a rapid decline of population between 1300 and 1450, losing more than one-half of its population.

2. *Pestilence*

The great plague of the fourteenth century, a pandemic called the Black Death, was carried to Europe from the East in 1347. Cities were struck repeatedly during the century, often losing more than half their populations. The Black Death was probably a pneumonic plague rather than the bubonic plague, but the high death rate is difficult to explain.

3. *Hunger*

Probably because of an overexpansion of population between 1000 and 1300, Europe suffered from a series of famines in the fourteenth century. Combined with disease and plague, hunger added to the loss of population.

4. Economic Effects

The economic consequences were both negative and positive. Pessimism discouraged economic effort, but the resulting shortage of labor encouraged the development of more efficient routines and of capital investment.

5. Agriculture

Prices are indicative of economic forces. After the Black Death, prices rose and remained high until the end of the fourteenth century, indicating falling production. In the fifteenth century, prices declined, wages rose, and diets improved. Sheep raising grew at a particularly rapid rate, encouraging English landlords to increase their land holdings, switch from crop raising, and expel peasants who lived on the land (enclosure). By the middle of the fifteenth century prices stabilized and agriculture had attained a new, more diversified stability.

II. Depression and Recovery in Trade and Industry

1. Protectionism

Entrepreneurs faced rapidly increasing wages. Efforts to secure effective governmental intervention to control wages and prices (the Statute of Laborers) failed. To control competition, entrepreneurs and cities restricted markets and established monopolies by limiting imports and forming guilds and monopolistic trade associations (Hanseatic League).

2. The Forces of Recovery

Hard times and labor shortages inspired technical advances.

3. Metallurgy

After 1460 there was a series of important inventions in mining, smelting, working, and casting of metals. Silver and iron production expanded dramatically, especially in Central Europe.

4. Firearms

Firearms, such as cannons, came into use during the fourteenth century, another example of substituting capital for labor.

5. Printing

The replacement of parchments by paper and the invention of printing with movable metal type by Johannes Gutenberg (the Gutenberg Bible, 1455) multiplied the output and cut the price of books. Reading would no longer be a monopoly of the rich and the clergy, and ideas could be spread with unprecedented speed.

6. Navigation

Larger ships and a variety of technical developments—such as the stern rudder, the Alfonsine Tables, the compass, and the *portolani* (port descriptions)—gave European mariners a mastery of Atlantic costal waters.

7. Business Institutions

Mercantile houses, such as the Medici bank of Florence (1397–1498), became more flexible through a system of interlocked partnerships. Banking was modernized by book transfers (an ancestor of the modern check) and double-entry bookkeeping (especially in Italy). Maritime insurance became common, encouraging investments in shipping.

8. The Economy in the Late Fifteenth Century

Europe, though a much smaller community, was more productive and richer than ever, thanks to increased diversification, capitalization, and rationalization in economic matters.

III. Popular Unrest

During the fourteenth and fifteenth centuries peasants and artisans revolted against the propertied classes many times.

1. Rural Revolts

The most prominent fourteenth-century rural uprising was the English Peasants' War of 1381. Angered by efforts of the government to limit wages and increase taxes—and by attempts of landlords to revive feudal dues—peasants, supported by urban workers, marched on London. After gaining apparent concessions from King Richard II, they were violently suppressed by the great landlords. Other revolts occurred throughout Europe into the sixteenth century.

2. Urban Revolts

For similar reasons, poor people revolted in cities throughout Europe. The temporarily successful Ciompi uprising at Florence (1378) revealed urban class tensions that would disturb capitalistic society in future centuries.

3. The Seeds of Discontent

The discontent that led to revolts did not come from people living in desperate poverty, but rather from people who were making economic gains and were thus in a stronger bargaining position. Moreover, psychological tensions accompanying plagues, famines, and wars gave people the emotional energy to take extreme actions. By 1450 a new stability was emerging. Most workers enjoyed higher wages, cheaper bread, and a better standard of living than before, as reflected in renewed population growth.

IV. The Governments of Europe

Protracted violence during the period reflected a weakening of governmental systems.

1. The Feudal Equilibrium

The balance of shared responsibilities that characterized governments was broken in the fourteenth century and had to be rebuilt.

2. Dynastic Instability

Dynasties in France, England, and elsewhere failed to perpetuate themselves, leading to wars (the Hundred Years' War, the English War of the Roses) between competing successors to the crown.

3. Fiscal Pressures

The costs of war went up, thanks to the increasing use of firearms and to mercenaries, while traditional revenues sank. Kings imposed new national taxes (on salt, hearths, individuals, windows), which led to conflicts of authority with assemblies, such as the Parliament in England and the Estates General in France.

4. Factional Conflicts

Many nobles suffered from the economic dislocations of the times. Attempting to improve their positions, they tended to coalesce into factions, disputing with each other over control of the government or distribution of its favors. This factional warfare throughout Europe constantly disturbed the peace.

5. England, France, and the Hundred Years' War

The greatest struggle of the epoch, the Hundred Years' War between France and England, was apparently fought over succession to the French throne. Yet more important was the clash of French and English interests in the cloth-making county of Flanders and the friction over competing claims to Aquitaine and Ponthieu. This war between Edward III of England and Philip of France was rooted in a breakdown of France's medieval feudal constitution.

6. The Tides of Battle

In this confused struggle, England was initially victorious (1338–1360); France enjoyed a resurgence, and then there was a stalemate from 1367 to 1415. England then rallied and, under Henry V, was on the verge of complete victory over the Dauphin (the future Charles VII) at Orléans.

7. Joan of Arc

A mystically inspired peasant girl, Joan of Arc, saved the French Capetian dynasty by turning the tide at Orléans and ensuring the coronation of the

Dauphin at Reims. A growing loyalty to the king led to a series of French successes followed by the execution of Joan in 1431, eliminating England as a continental power by 1453.

8. The Effects of the Hundred Years' War

The war confirmed the supremacy of the infantry over mounted knights. In England, the need for new taxes strengthened Parliament at the expense of royal power. In France, new taxes (the *gabelle,* or salt tax) helped establish royal domination over the fiscal system. Both countries suffered from factional struggles. In England, the Lancastrians and Yorkists warred with each other for 35 years (the War of the Roses), until Henry VII (Tudor) defeated the Yorkists in 1485. In France, the struggle between Armagnacs and Burgundians finally ended under Charles VII, thanks, in part, to the creation of Europe's first standing professional army since Rome. For a while, Burgundy threatened to establish a strong "middle kingdom" between France and the Holy Roman Empire, but the death of its last duke in 1477 brought that threat to an end. England had thus stabilized and consolidated itself, while France's king gained power and prestige.

9. The Holy Roman Empire

The Holy Roman Empire was no longer a major European power. The emperors were generally more concerned with the interests of the Habsburg dynasty. They were subject to the Golden Bull (1356), which provided for the election of the emperor by seven powerful German electors. Late in the thirteenth century, the governments of Swiss cantons confederated to form an exception to the trend toward centralized governments.

10. The States of Italy

In the north and center of Italy, self-governing city-states dominated political life at the beginning of the fourteenth century. Factional rivalries, economic contraction, and rising military costs combined to weaken these smaller governments. Strong, sometimes despotic governments and regional states replaced them. Gian Galeazzo Visconti (1378–1402), who expanded Milan into a major regional power, is a good example of a powerful despotic ruler. Venice, under a kind of corporative despot (the Council of Ten), similarly expanded its territories. The banker Cosimo de Medici rose to power in Florence; under his rule and that of his grandson, Lorenzo the Magnificent (1469–1492), Florence—with its festivals, social life, buildings, and cultural community—set the style for Italy and, eventually, for Europe.

11. The Papal States and the Kingdom of Naples

In the papal states in central Italy, popes had difficulty asserting effective control. Political chaos also reigned in the Kingdom of Naples and Sicily until 1435, when the king of Aragon, Alfonso V, unified them.

12. Diplomacy

By 1450 Italy was divided among the Duchy of Milan, the republics of Venice and Florence, the Papal States, and the Kingdom of Naples. Thanks to new diplomatic methods and to the Peace of Lodi (1454), the Italian states developed an effective balance-of-power system that maintained peace for the next 40 years.

V. The Papacy

Powerful forces beset the papacy, weakening its authority and influence.

1. The Avignon Exile

From 1308 to 1377 popes resided in Avignon, a French-speaking independent state in southern France.

2. Fiscal Crisis

Lacking sufficient territorial resources for financial requirements, popes used their powers to make appointments, grant dispensations, collect tithes, and grant indulgences to raise funds. Though financially successful, the practices were unpopular and helped create chaos in many parts of the Western Church.

3. The Great Schism

Political struggles between the French and Italian factions led to the election of two, and later three, popes between 1378 and 1417. Europe split its support between the popes, each collecting his own taxes and excommunicating everyone on the other side.

4. The Conciliar Movement

Theologians and jurists argued that the Church should be governed by a general council, thereby reducing the pope's role. Their ideas turned into a movement during the schism, and at the Council of Constance (1414–1418) the views of the conciliarists prevailed. But the movement proved to be impractical, as revealed at the Council of Basel (1431–1449). It ended with the election of Nicholas V. Meanwhile, monarchs throughout Europe exerted greater control over their territorial churches, evidencing a deterioration of papal control over the international Christian community.

5. The Revival of Rome

In Rome the popes rebuilt their office and prestige, adopting the cultural ideas of the Renaissance and militarily establishing the papacy as a major Italian power. But they were losing the spiritual allegiance of Europe, especially in the north.

GUIDE TO DOCUMENTS

Boccaccio on the Black Death

1. What assumptions about disease during this period are revealed in this document? What efforts were made to deal with it?
2. What might be the consequences of these facts reported by Boccaccio?

The Trial of Joan of Arc

1. How does this help explain the power and influence of Joan of Arc?
2. What does this reveal about legal methods during these times, particularly in these sorts of cases?

The Papacy Condemns Conciliarism

1. How does the pope justify his power?
2. As revealed by this document, what sorts of challenges to its authority were faced by the papacy during the fifteenth century?

SIGNIFICANT INDIVIDUALS

Political Leaders

Wat Tyler (14th century), English peasant leader.

Jack Straw (14th century), English peasant leader.

John Ball (14th century), English peasant leader.

Henry VII (1458–1509), king of England.

Philip the Bold (1363–1414), duke of Burgundy.

Gian Galeazzo Visconti (1378–1402), ruler of Milan.

Cosimo de Medici (1389–1464), banker, ruler of Florence.

Lorenzo the Magnificent (1469–1492), Medici ruler of Florence.

Religious Leaders

Martin V (1417–1431), pope.

Nicholas V (1447–1455), pope.

Cultural Figures

Johannes Gutenberg (1400?–1468), German inventor.

Aldus Manutius (1450–1515), Venetian printer.

CHRONOLOGICAL DIAGRAM

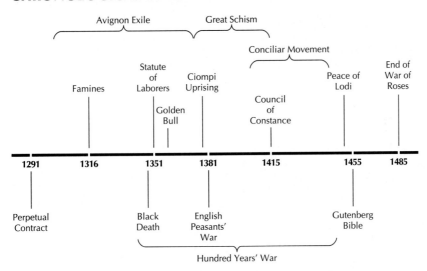

IDENTIFICATION

Black Death
enclosure
Statute of Laborers
Hanseatic League
Alfonsine Tables
Golden Bull
Peace of Lodi
Great Schism

double-entry bookkeeping
English Peasants' War
Ciompi uprising
War of the Roses
the *gabelle*
conciliar movement
council of constance

MAP EXERCISES

1. Label the five major states of Italy in 1454.

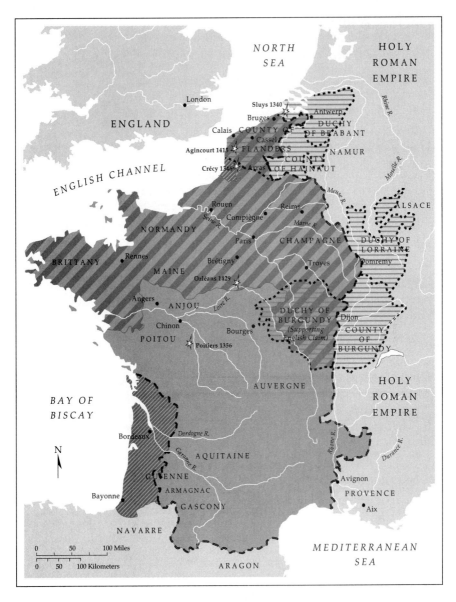

1. Indicate areas controlled by France, Burgundy, and England in 1339, in 1429, and in 1500.

PROBLEMS FOR ANALYSIS

I. *Population Disaster and Agricultural Change*

1. What were the main developments that characterized the economic and demographic disasters of the fourteenth and fifteenth centuries? How can these developments best be explained?

II. *Depression and Recovery in Trade and Industry*

1. Considering the loss of population, the technical advances, and the innovations in business institutions, was the long-term effect of the depression and demographic decline economically beneficial? Why?

III. *Popular Unrest*

1. Analyze the governmental policies, the economic circumstances, and the psychological tensions that led to the rural and urban revolts of the fourteenth century. Was desperate poverty a primary cause?

IV. *The Governments of Europe*

1. In what ways was the feudal equilibrium in government broken in the fourteenth century? How is this illustrated by the Hundred Years' War?
2. Compare political development in the Holy Roman Empire with that in France or England.
3. In what ways were the states of Italy able to gain relative stability during the fifteenth century?

V. *The Papacy*

1. Explain how the Avignon exile, the Great Schism, and the conciliar movement contributed to the weakening of the Church and, especially, papal authority. How did the papacy's secular concerns contribute to this?

SPECULATIONS

1. Suppose you were one of the popes during the Great Schism. How would you explain the Great Schism, and what policies would you follow? Why?
2. If England had been more successful militarily in the Hundred Years' Wars, do you think it might have maintained control over much of France for a long time? Why?
3. If a series of plagues and famines struck this country today, how do you think the people would react? What would the consequences be? Do you think there would be an experience parallel to that in fourteenth-century Europe? Why?

TRANSITIONS

In "The Crusades and Eastern Europe," connections between the West and East were examined in light of the decline of Byzantium, the rise of the Ottomans, and the formation of modern Russia.

In "The West in Transition: Economy and Institutions," it was seen that Europe suffered a temporary decline. Compared with the thirteenth century, population decreased, political instability spread, wars proliferated, and papal authority disintegrated. Yet Europe would recover and gain new dynamism by the second half of the fifteenth century. The period between the middle of the fourteenth and the fifteenth centuries should be considered both an autumn and a renaissance for Europe.

In "The West in Transition: Society and Culture," the culture, values, and society of that same period will be examined.

TWELVE
THE WEST IN TRANSITION:
SOCIETY AND CULTURE

MAIN THEMES

1. The culture of the Renaissance was first produced within the dynamic society of Italian cities.
2. Humanism was at the core of Renaissance culture.
3. The visual arts came to most vividly represent Humanism. Art and artists gained a new status among the elite.
4. In the last quarter of the fifteenth century Humanism came to the north, where the culture of the times emphasized chivalry, the cult of decay, and pietism.
5. Foundations for later scientific developments were formed during this period. An analytical and pietistic approach characterized religious developments, particularly in the north.

OUTLINE AND SUMMARY

I. *Italian Society*

In the fourteenth and fifteenth centuries Italian society produced a cultural Renaissance.

1. *Cities*

Italy was more highly urbanized than other areas of Europe. Its urban population was unusually well educated and active in economic and political affairs.

2. *Families*

Italian families were distinctively small (fewer than four persons per household); males were usually much older than their young brides. This demographic pattern led to a surplus of unmarried women and a low birthrate, which in turn attracted ambitious immigrants to the cities. Women dominated family life, and children became of extraordinary concern.

3. *Life Expectancy*

Mortality levels were high during the fourteenth and fifteenth centuries. Life expectancy averaged 30 years, except during the Black Death, when it dropped to 18. This increased opportunities for young people willing to experiment to rise in society and influence the style and ideas of the times.

4. Florence and Venice

Italy's two richest cities, Florence and Venice, were the most important centers of Renaissance culture. Florence, economically based on its banking and production of luxury goods, was generally run by its wealthy families but was politically unstable. Venice—relying on its armed forces, its ship building, and its trade with the East—enjoyed political stability under its patricians.

II. The New Learning

Scholastic education seemed inappropriate for laypeople interested in business, politics, and practical ethics.

1. Humanism

By the late thirteenth century an intellectual movement, Humanism, was founded in Italian cities. Humanism stressed moral philosophy and eloquence, Latin and Classical writings, and human perfection through new learning and traditional religious piety.

    a. *Petrarch:* Petrarch was the most influential early humanist, writing poetry, scholarly and moral treatises, and letters. He emulated Latin and Classical writings and stressed imitation of Classical figures for moral betterment.

    b. *Boccaccio:* The Florentine Boccaccio became a supporter of Petrarch's ideas and author of *The Decameron,* a collection of short stories.

2. The Civic Humanists

This group of Florentine scholars, led by Coluccio Salutati, instituted a movement to recover antiquity—particularly through the command of the Greek language. They argued for training in the classics, participation in public affairs (*vita activa*), and support of Florentine republican institutions.

3. Humanism in the Fifteenth Century

Humanism spread from Florence to other Italian cities; political leaders patronized the humanists. Guarino da Verona and Vittorino da Feltre created a humanistic curriculum and instituted humanistic educational ideas ("Happy House"). A humanistic education became important for the elite and a sign of social prestige as revealed in Castiglione's *The Courtier* (1516). Schools, universities, and the new printing press spread humanistic ideas.

4. The Florentine Neoplatonists

A group of influential Florentine philosophers, most notably Marsilio Ficino and Pico della Mirandola, attempted to reconcile Platonic philosophy and Christian belief. They argued that a person should strive for personal perfection and contemplate the beautiful (*vita contemplativa*).

5. The Heritage of Humanism

Italian humanists utilized the past—through linguistic skills, historical criticism, and philosophical speculation—to guide people in the present. They addressed themselves, through their writings and their schools, to lay society. Their work profoundly influenced Western culture.

III. Art and Artists in the Italian Renaissance

Humanism strongly affected the visual arts, first in Florence—already a leader (Cimabue and Giotto), extraordinarily wealthy, and full of skilled designers from the luxury goods trades.

1. Three Friends

The painter Masaccio, the sculptor Donatello, and the architect Brunelleschi were the great pioneers in applying Humanism to art. Other artists followed the pattern of these pioneers, particularly in their imitation of Roman models.

2. The High Renaissance

High Renaissance Italian art (early 1500s) is best represented by Leonardo, Raphael, Michelangelo, and Titian. Leonardo was extraordinarily experimental and versatile (*Mona Lisa, Last Supper*). Raphael emphasized harmony, beauty, and serenity (*The School of Athens*). Michelangelo's sculptures and paintings were extraordinarily dynamic. Titians paintings were unusually sensuous, and his portraits were much sought-after.

3. Status and Perception

Art gained recognition as the most vivid manifestation of the humanist movement. Artists sought and gained fame and personal prestige from their accomplishments. A new attitude demanded that princes acquire lasting prestige by cultivating both the fine and the martial arts. The status of artists was transformed as they became prizes at aristocratic courts such as those of the Medici. Vasari wrote the first history of art, arguing that the new status of the artist was well deserved.

IV. The Culture of the North

In the north, more distant from the monuments of antiquity in Italy and less urbanized, the court and the knight dominated culture; Humanism did not come until the last quarter of the fifteenth century.

1. Chivalry

A lingering of medieval civilization and an emotional distortion of reality, which characterized northern culture, are reflected in the idealization of the knight, with his inflated notions of battle and romance.

2. The Cult of Decay

The north was a psychologically disturbed and religiously unsettled world at the time. Themes of death, decay, and demonology dominated its culture, though other trends were also present.

3. Contemporary Views of Northern Society

Observers of northern society included Jean Froissart, who depicted chivalric society; William Langland, who in *Vision of Piers Plowman* commented more broadly on medieval society; and Geoffrey Chaucer, who summed up the moral and social ills of his times in *Canterbury Tales*.

4. The Fine Arts

Jan Van Eyck exemplified the realistic detail and piety of northern painting. Albrecht Dürer displayed similar qualities in his highly popular engravings.

5. Music

Musicians became prizes as artists at princely courts. New methods of musical notation and a variety of musical instruments were invented and employed, above all in the Low Countries.

V. Scholastic Philosophy, Religious Thought, and Piety

Thinkers of the fourteenth and fifteenth centuries were more concerned with analytical thought and piety than thirteenth-century Scholastics.

1. The "Modern Way"

William of Ockham was the most prominent of a group of philosophers who believed in nominalism. Ockham argued that the most simple explanation, based on direct experience, is the best way to understand reality. This comparatively pessimistic but popular philosophy, which as a theology emphasized the power of God, came to be known as the *via moderna* ("modern way").

2. Social and Scientific Thought

Marsilius of Padua (*Defender of Peace*) and others influenced by nominalism criticized the papal and clerical domination of Western political life by formulating radical ideas about political sovereignty. In the fourteenth century nominalists, such as Jean Buridan, questioned Aristotle and established a basis for later scientific advances. The humanistic tradition of criticism, care, and precision also contributed to later scientific developments.

3. Styles of Piety

The consolations of mystical piety, formerly restricted to monastic orders, spread through literature and religious guilds to laypeople.

4. Female Piety

Piety among the laity was particularly apparent among women. More women joined religious groups outside convents.

5. The Mystics

A number of figures in the Rhine valley—such as Meister Eckhart, Gerhard Groote, and Thomas à Kempis (*The Imitation of Christ*)—stressed emotional communion with God and simple humility in everyday life. Their teachings, known as *devotio moderna* ("modern devotion"), spread through a religious congregation (the Brethren of the Common Life) and its schools. This lay piety was a striking contrast to the formal ritualism and Scholasticism of the thirteenth century.

6. Movements of Doctrinal Reform

Reform movements attacked religious establishments within the Church. Charismatic leaders such as John Wycliffe (Lollards) and Jan Hus (Hussites) revolted against the Church and some of its doctrines, anticipating the concerns of later Protestantism, such as predestination.

GUIDE TO DOCUMENTS

Petrarch on Ancient Rome

1. What qualities of his own age bother Petrarch?
2. What does he find preferable about Roman times?
3. In what ways does Petrarch reflect the concerns of Italian Humanism?

Isabella d'Este's Quest for Art

1. What does this document reveal about patrons' motives for acquiring art during the Renaissance?
2. What concerns and demands faced leading artists of the Renaissance such as Bellini and Leonardo da Vinci?

Hus at Constance

1. What sort of inspiration and leadership does Hus offer his followers?
2. Why might Hus be considered so dangerous to Church authorities?

SIGNIFICANT INDIVIDUALS

Italian Humanists

Francesco Petrarch (1304–1373), writer.

Giovanni Boccaccio (1313–1375), writer.

Coluccio Salutati (14th century),
   civic humanist.
Lorenzo Valla (1407–1457), writer.

Vittorino de Feltre (1378–1446),
   educator.

Scholars and Philosophers

Marsilio Ficino (1433–1499),
   Florentine Neoplatonist.
Pico della Mirandola (1463–1494),
   Florentine Neoplatonist.

William of Ockham (1300–1349?),
   English nominalist.
Marsilius of Padua (1290?–1343),
   Italian.

Religious Reformers

Meister Eckhart (1260?–1327),
   Rhenish preacher.
Gerhard Grotte (1340–1383),
   Rhenish reformer.
Thomas à Kempis (1380–1471),
   German religious writer.

John Wycliffe (1320?–1384),
   English heretic.
Jan Hus (1369–1415), Czech
   heretic.

Painters

Giotto (1276?–1337), Florentine.
Masaccio (1401–1428), Florentine.
Jan Van Eyck (1385–1440),
   Flemish.
Raphael Santi (1483–1520), Italian.

Leonardo da Vinci (1452–1520),
   Italian.
Michelangelo Buonarroti (1475–
   1564), Italian painter, sculptor,
   architect.

CHRONOLOGICAL DIAGRAM

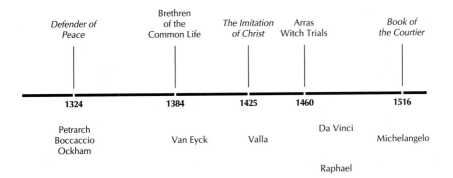

IDENTIFICATION

civic Humanism
Casa Giocosa (Happy House)
Neoplatonism
chivalry
vita contemplativa
the Brethren of the Common Life

Ockham's razor
nominalism
lay piety
Lollards
Hussites

MAP EXERCISE

1. Circle the main centers of the Italian Renaissance discussed in the book.

PROBLEMS FOR ANALYSIS

I. Italian Society

1. What role did demographic patterns, and particularly family life, play in the development of the Renaissance in Italian cities?

II. The New Learning

1. What are the main characteristics of Italian Humanism? How do these compare with earlier medieval Scholasticism? Why were Italian humanists so interested in Classical civilization?

III. Art and Artists in the Italian Renaissance

1. In what ways did art change in the Renaissance?
2. In what ways did the role of the artist and the prestige attached to art change? Why was this so important?
3. Compare Italian and northern art.

IV. The Culture of the North

1. What social and historical factors help explain the differences between the culture of the north and the culture of Italy?
2. Is it fair to argue that the culture of the north was one of pessimism and decay, a holdover from the Middle Ages? Why?

V. Scholastic Philosophy, Religious Thought, and Piety

1. Compare the analytical religious thought of nominalists, such as William of Ockham, with the synthetic Scholasticism of Thomas Aquinas.
2. Was mystical piety a rejection of the teachings of the medieval Church?
3. In what ways were foundations for later scientific developments created in the fourteenth and fifteenth centuries?

SPECULATIONS

1. The fourteenth and fifteenth centuries have been described as a period of political, economic, and social turmoil and disaster. Yet, it was also a period of extraordinary cultural creativity. How can you explain this apparent contradiction?
2. Considering his designs for the airplane, tank, and submarine, should Leonardo da Vinci be considered as important as an inventor as he was an artist? Why?
3. How do you imagine a noble from one of the northern courts would react upon visiting Florence in the mid-fourteenth century? Why?

TRANSITIONS

In "The West in Transition: Economy and Institutions," the economic depressions, social disasters, political instability, and religious disunity of the fourteenth and fifteenth centuries were examined. The picture at that period was gloomy compared to the thirteenth century.

In "The West in Transition: Society and Culture," we see that the same period was also one of extraordinary cultural creativity. In Italy a humanistic and artistic culture, responding to the new social needs of the dominant literate lay aristocracy, grew. In the north a more conservative and pietistic culture, clinging to the ideals of chivalry still prevalent among the lay aristocracy but nevertheless borrowing from Italian culture, evolved.

In "Reformations in Religion," the great religious upheavals that destroyed religious unity in the West will be analyzed.

THIRTEEN
REFORMATIONS
IN RELIGION

MAIN THEMES

1. Discontent with the Church and a growing demand for spiritual consolation combined to set the stage for the Reformation. Northern humanists, such as Thomas More and Erasmus, combined themes of Italian Humanism with religious concerns, creating an intellectual environment for the Reformation.
2. Lutheranism, based upon the doctrine of justification by faith and the idea that the Bible was the sole religious authority, grew within the politically divided Holy Roman Empire.
3. Zwingli and Calvin led new reform movements, and other groups, such as the Anabaptists and the Melchiorites, led more radical breaks from established religion.
4. Led by Pope Paul III, the Council of Trent, and the Jesuits, the Catholic Church reformed itself and initiated a revival of Catholicism.

OUTLINE AND SUMMARY

I. *Piety and Dissent*

1. *Doctrine*

By 1500 the Church was increasingly stressing the institutional path to salvation, while reformers within the Church had been stressing the inward path to salvation.

2. *Forms of Piety*

Demand grew for more personal spiritual consolation, as evidenced by the emphasis on personal piety, the growth of mystical and lay religious fraternities (the Brotherhood of the Eleven Thousand Virgins in Germany), and the ascendancy of Savonarola in Florence. The Church ignored demands for reform, except in Spain under Cardinal Ximenes.

3. *The Legacy of Wycliffe and Hus*

Protest movements by groups such as the Lollards in England and the Hussites in Germany revealed great dissatisfaction with Church teachings.

4. Causes of Discontent

The spiritual authority of the Church seemed to be declining, as evidenced by the Babylonian captivity in Avignon, the Great Schism, the secularization of the papacy and clergy, the growth of anticlericalism, and the failure of the Church to meet the needs of people longing for personal salvation.

5. Popular Religion

In villages people listened to itinerant preachers emphasizing the power of faith. Religious issues were regularly discussed, particularly in evening meetings (the *veillée*). Popular piety was growing.

6. The Impact of Printing

Thanks to the invention of the printing press, new religious ideas spread and people became less dependent on the clergy for biblical material.

7. Piety and Protest in Literature and Art

The popularity of critical literature (Rabelais, broadsides) and the prevalence of spiritual themes in the work of northern artists (Bosch, Grünewald, and Dürer) reveal the dissatisfaction with the Church and the concern for individual spiritual values in Europe.

8. Christian Humanism

Humanists in northern centers such as the University of Heidelberg used humanistic methods to examine religious issues and analyze early Christianity.

9. More and Erasmus

Thomas More and Erasmus were the most famous of the Christian humanists. More argued in *Utopia* that a religious person should participate in society, and that society could promote the truly Christian life if properly organized and based on ascetic Christian principles. Erasmus strove for common sense and a revival of early, pure Christian faith based upon the life of Jesus. His biblical translations, books (*The Praise of Folly*), and letters were very influential, yet he refused to join either the Protestant or the Catholic side in the growing struggle.

II. The Lutheran Reformation

1. The Conditions for Change

The religious and political environment of the Holy Roman Empire was well-suited to the success of a determined reformer, such as Martin Luther.

2. Martin Luther

After experiencing personal crises and wrestling with a continuing sense of sinfulness, and despite almost superhuman efforts to lead a worthy monastic and scholarly life, Martin Luther came upon an insight that would become the core of his thinking: that justification is achieved by faith alone.

3.   The Indulgence Controversy

In 1517 Luther publicly challenged a Dominican monk, Tetzel, for selling indulgences (the 95 theses). Over the next three years, this act and subsequent publications brought Luther into conflict with the Dominicans and the pope.

4.   The Diet of Worms

The pope excommunicated the defiant Luther. The Holy Roman Emperor, Charles V, condemned Luther at the Diet of Worms, but Luther was saved by a politically independent German prince, Elector Frederick III of Saxony.

5.   Lutheran Doctrine and Practice

Luther and Melanchton codified Lutheranism in the Augsburg Confession (1530). The two fundamental assertions, partially derived from earlier nominalism, were that the individual could be justified by faith alone—not good works or the sacraments—and that the Bible was the sole religious authority—not tradition or pronouncements. The importance of priests or any intermediaries was diminished, most of the sacraments were denied, celibacy was rejected, the Mass was altered, ritual was simplified, and the laity was encouraged to read the translated version of the Bible.

6.   The Spread of Lutheranism

Luther immediately gained a following as well as political support, but at the same time, more radical reformers and doctrines arose that Luther strongly opposed.

7.   Disorder and Revolt

In 1522, a revolt of imperial knights in the name of Lutheranism was crushed. In 1525 Luther opposed a peasant uprising in the name of political and social order and made bolder attacks on Catholics and Jews.

8.   Lutheranism Established

Luther may have saved himself and his religion by siding with politically powerful princes. His conservatism appealed to the princes, who had religious, economic, and political reasons for becoming Lutheran. By 1529 Lutheran princes had allied formally, and by midcentury, after war over religion had broken out, approximately half the population of the Holy Roman Empire was Lutheran. Despite military losses, the Protestants gained a compromise allowing each ruler to determine the religion of his territory (Diet at Augsburg, 1555). Lutheranism went on to influence fundamental assumptions of European life.

III. The Growth of Protestantism

1. Zwinglianism

From Zurich, Ulrich Zwingli led a successful reform movement in parts of the Swiss Confederation in the 1520s. He emphasized simplicity, individualism, the need to educate and discipline all, the unimportance of mystery and ritual, and the lack of distinction between secular and religious authority. Although there were many similarities with Lutheranism, the two men could not agree on doctrine. Civil war broke out between Swiss Catholics and followers of Zwingli (1531). Zwingli was killed. Eventually his following was reduced, but it did influence other forms of Protestantism.

2. The Radicals

Several radical sects, such as the Anabaptists, formed, some establishing utopian communities.

3. Persecution

Established Lutheran and Zwinglian churches, like the Catholics, were intolerant of the radicals. In the 1520s and 1530s groups such as the Melchiorites in Münster were assaulted and persecuted.

4. John Calvin

John Calvin (*Institutes of the Christian Religion*) developed a systematic and dynamic form of Protestantism in the 1540s.

5. Calvinism

In most matters, Calvinism resembled Lutheranism but stressed the overwhelming power of God, predestination, the union of secular and religious authority, and the importance of hierarchy and structure within the Church. From their base in Geneva, organized disciplines with missionary zeal spread Calvinism to Scotland and parts of England, Germany, Switzerland, France, the Low Countries, and Hungary. It was particularly appealing in cities and in many areas among women.

IV. The Catholic Revival

1. Reform and Counter Reform

In the 1530s, in part as a reaction to the Protestant Reformation and in part as an internal movement, the Catholic Church started to purify itself. Most Europeans remained Catholic.

2. Crisis and Change in the Church

Pope Paul III deserves much of the credit for the revival of the Catholic Church. Between 1534 and 1549 he set into motion a major church council to reexamine traditional theology, founded a Roman Inquisition to uproot heresy, attacked abuses within the Church, appointed cardinals of high quality, and paved the way for the succession of unusually successful popes.

3. The Council of Trent

At the ecumenical council at Trent (1545–1563) religious doctrine was debated and finally established, vigorously affirming the traditional Catholic position on most matters. Its policies were in striking contrast to the austerity, sternness, and predestination stressed by the Protestants. The council adjusted the Church to the world.

4. The Aftermath of Trent

There was a strong revival of Catholic faith, particularly among leaders and artists. Women's orders played a key role in the revival of Catholicism, particularly in Spain as evidenced by the order founded by St. Teresa. The popes and their diplomats struggled everywhere against Protestantism.

5. Ignatius Loyola

Loyola, after having a deeply moving religious experience, dedicated himself to a religious life within the Catholic Church. In his great work, *Spiritual Exercises,* he emphasized absolute discipline and the efficacy of free will and good works for attaining personal grace. In 1540 the papacy approved his plans for the founding of a new order, the Jesuits.

6. The Jesuits

Through preaching, hearing confessions, teaching, and founding missions, the extremely knowledgeable, talented, and disciplined followers of Loyola gained tremendous success in stemming the tide of Protestantism. In many cases they returned great numbers into the Catholic fold. Jesuits established the most respected schools in Europe, gained considerable influence in important courts, and conducted successful missionary projects.

7. Religion and Politics

Struggles over politics and religion entwined in wars of great ferocity.

GUIDE TO DOCUMENTS

Luther's "Experience in the Tower"

1. In light of this document, what does "justification by faith" mean, according to Luther?
2. Why might an experience like this be so crucial to someone like Luther?

The Trial of Elizabeth Dirks

1. What teachings of the Roman Catholic Church does Elizabeth Dirks reject here? Why might her beliefs be viewed as so threatening to the Roman Catholic Church?
2. What does this excerpt reveal about the beliefs that led Elizabeth Dirks and perhaps others to join radical groups during the Reformation?

St. Teresa's Visions

1. What does this excerpt reveal about the appeal of faith and mystical visions within sixteenth-century Catholicism?
2. Why might some readers of the autobiography of St. Teresa find these passages so inspiring?

SIGNIFICANT INDIVIDUALS

Reformers and Protestants

Savonarola (1452–1498), Italian religious reformer.

Martin Luther (1483–1546), German Protestant.

Philipp Melanchton (1497–1546), German Protestant.

Ulrich Zwingli (1484–1531), Swiss Protestant.

John Calvin (1509–1564), French, Swiss Protestant.

Catholics

Paul III (1468–1549), reforming pope.

Ignatius Loyola (1491–1556), Spanish founder of the Jesuits.

Francis Xavier (1506–1552), Jesuit missionary.

Humanists

François Rabelais (1494?–1553), French.

Sir Thomas More (1478–1535), English.

Desiderius Erasmus (1466?–1536), Dutch.

Artists

Hieronymus Bosch (1450–1516), Dutch painter.

Albrecht Dürer (1471–1528), German engraver.

Matthias Grünewald (1500–1530), German painter.

CHRONOLOGICAL DIAGRAM

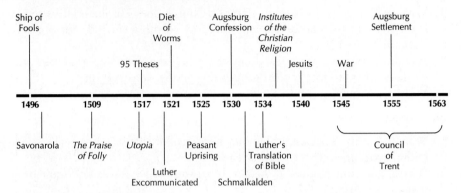

IDENTIFICATION

lay religious fraternities
village gatherings
printing press
Utopia
justification by faith
indulgences
95 theses
Index of Forbidden Books

Jesuits
Diet of Worms
priesthood of all believers
Augsburg Confession
predestination
Melchiorites
Council of Trent
good works

MAP EXERCISE

1. Indicate the main Lutheran, Calvinist, and Anglican areas in the late 1500s.

PROBLEMS FOR ANALYSIS

I. Piety and Dissent

1. What were the sources of religious discontent that preceded the Reformation? What evidence is there for this?
2. Compare northern and Italian Humanism.
3. In what ways is it appropriate to focus on Thomas More and Erasmus and representatives of northern Humanism?

II. The Lutheran Reformation

1. What were the main differences in doctrine and practice between Catholicism and Lutheranism?
2. "Despite his revolutionary actions, Martin Luther was quite authoritarian and conservative." Do you agree? Explain.

III. The Growth of Protestantism

1. "Protestantism was not simply a single movement away from the Roman Catholic Church; it was a series of separate and often conflicting movements." Do you agree? Explain.
2. Why did Calvinism develop into the most dynamic of the Protestant forces during the mid-sixteenth century?

IV. The Catholic Revival

1. In what ways was the Catholic revival of the sixteenth century both a Counter Reformation and a Catholic Reformation?
2. How did Pope Paul III, the Council of Trent, and the Jesuits contribute to the Catholic revival?

SPECULATIONS

1. Suppose you were the pope in 1515 but had the hindsight of a historian living in the 1990s. What might you have done to prevent the Reformation? Do you think your efforts would have had a good chance of succeeding?
2. How important was Martin Luther to the Reformation? Do you think the Reformation would have occurred without him?
3. Which do you think was more compatible with the Renaissance and the secular developments of the early sixteenth century, Catholicism or Protestantism? Explain.

TRANSITIONS

In "The West in Transition: Society and Culture," the dynamic cultural developments of the fourteenth and fifteenth centuries and the social conditions supporting those developments were examined.

In "Reformations in Religion," the shattering of religious unity in Europe during the first half of the sixteenth century is analyzed. The fundamental religious issue of the Reformation was how sinful humans could gain salvation. Increasingly, the Catholic Church answered this question by emphasizing the role of the Church. Reformers reversed this trend by emphasizing the inward and personal approach. But spiritual conflict quickly evolved into fanatical attacks on all sides; moderation and tolerance failed almost everywhere.

In "Economic Expansion and a New Politics," Europe experiences a political, economic, and geographic revival characterized by the growth of monarchical power, commercial growth, and overseas expansion.

FOURTEEN
ECONOMIC EXPANSION
AND A NEW POLITICS

MAIN THEMES

1. In the sixteenth century, Europe experienced population and economic growth. A series of social developments stemmed from these changes.
2. Europeans, led by the Portuguese and then by the Spaniards, expanded over the globe establishing empires over vast territories.
3. "New monarchs" in Western Europe increased their authority and power.
4. In parts of Eastern Europe and Italy, central authority was unable to overcome forces that were splintering areas into small, relatively autonomous units.
5. Initiated in Italy, new theories and practices of diplomacy and statecraft, focusing on the realities of power, spread throughout Europe.

OUTLINE AND SUMMARY

I. Expansion at Home

1. Population Increase

Between 1470 and 1620, Europe's population rose rapidly, particularly in the cities. Consequences of the population increase included a rise in food prices and enclosures in England.

2. Economic Growth

Trade expanded as did such industries as shipbuilding, glassmaking, and cloth. Large financial firms, such as the Fuggers, invested in trade and made close ties to leading monarchs. The guild system expanded, and the notion of a business enterprise as an abstract entity was established.

3. Inflation and Silver

Prices slowly inflated after 1500. Precious metals played an important role here, above all silver imports from the New World, but more important was a growth of demand.

150

4. The Commercial Revolution

New financial methods and the expansion of capitalist outlooks (accumulation of tangible wealth for its own sake) and practices came to dominate Europe's economy.

5. Social Change: The Countryside

Food producers and landowners benefited from economic prosperity, but wages lagged far behind prices. Combined with an increasing population, this created large numbers of rural and urban poor, who resorted to wandering, crime, and begging. During the seventeenth century governments established some institutions offering basic welfare benefits, although these were quite inadequate.

6. Social Change: The Town

Crime and disease plagued the urban poor more than the rural poor. But some were able to take advantage of economic opportunity in the cities. Women often took on new roles in the trades. Among the elite, some gained new wealth, title, and prestige; a new aristocracy was born.

II. Expansion Overseas

1. The Portuguese

In the fifteenth century, Prince Henry the Navigator of Portugal—motivated by a mixture of profit, religion, and curiosity—patronized a major effort of exploration and conquest. Eventually, Portuguese explorers, such as Bartholomeu Dias and Vasco da Gama, sailed around Africa, reached India, and made discoveries that would make Portugal the leader in the establishment of sea routes and trade with India and Asia. The Portuguese avoided colonization, establishing instead trading posts from Africa to China. Thus the West—supported by driving ambition, technical superiority in guns and ships, tactical skills, commercial expertise, and careful planning—began its rise to worldwide power. This expansion was continually sustained by competition among the various European states.

2. The Spaniards

Spain founded its empire on conquest and colonization. Explorers such as Christopher Columbus, Vasco da Balboa, and Ferdinand Magellan made the New World the focus of Spain's explorations and started a tradition of violence against local peoples. Conquistadors, such as Hernando Cortés and Francisco Pizarro, led Spanish troops to victory in Mexico and South America and turned the land over to Spanish administrators (viceroys).

3. The First Colonial Empire

Spanish viceroys dominated Spanish administration in the New World. Women pioneers enabled real growth of settlements to occur. Indigenous people were exploited and inhumanely treated. In 1545 silver was discovered in Bolivia, creating treasures that enriched Spain and, in turn, much of Europe.

4. The Life of the Settlers

Sea passage was difficult and dangerous as was life upon arrival. For all but the relatively few *hidalgos,* clergy, and officials, leaving Europe was a fairly desperate act, perhaps fueled by the population increase. Some governments used criminals and religious minorities to populate colonies. Indigenous populations were exploited and decimated. Slaves from Africa were shipped to the colonies, where those who survived would endure lives and generations of toil.

III. The Centralization of Political Power

1. The "New Monarchs"

During the late fifteenth and early sixteenth centuries monarchs in England, France, and Spain gained greater power.

2. Tudor England

English kings drew support from three sources: an effective administrative structure staffed by the powerful gentry, a strong but subordinate Parliament, and a uniform system of justice based upon common law.

3. Henry VII

Henry VII triumphed in the War of the Roses and founded the Tudor dynasty in 1485. By efficiently managing finances and restoring order, he increased royal authority.

4. Henry VIII and His Successors

Henry VIII was a much bolder king than his father. With the aid of his strong chief minister, Cardinal Wolsey, he gained military success and consolidated his royal power at home. The inability of Wolsey to obtain from the pope a divorce for Henry, who wanted a son, caused his downfall. His replacement, Thomas Cromwell, encouraged Henry to break with the pope and head the English Church himself. Henry did this in 1534, adding wealth to the crown through collection of ecclesiastical fees and sale of monastic lands. The ability of the king and Parliament to bring this about increased the power and prestige of both institutions. Attempts by the nobility to regain lost power under Edward VI (1547–1553) and the Catholic Mary I (1553–1558) were short-lived, as Elizabeth assumed power and increased monarchical authority.

5. Valois France

In the fifteenth century, France's administrative system was less centralized than England's. Its lands were larger, its nobles were stronger, and local representative assemblies were more independent. French kings, however, took advantage of taxes (*aide, taille, gabelle*) to support an increasingly costly but powerful standing army, and of Roman law to issue ordinances and edicts, thereby strengthening royal authority.

6. Louis XI and Charles VIII

Louis XI added to French power and territories by defeating the duke of Burgundy and annexing most of his vast lands (1477). Thanks to clever diplomacy and luck, he gained further territories in the south and elsewhere. Charles VIII continued the pattern but also initiated a series of wars in Italy (1494) that lasted for 65 years.

7. The Growth of Government Power

Although France was a rich country, governmental expenses were high; and nobles, many towns, royal officeholders, and clergy were exempt from some taxes. Louis XII (1498–1515) and Francis I (1515–1547) tried to solve this problem by selling administrative offices. This created new dynasties of noble officeholders, a new administrative class, and a growth of bureaucracies. In 1516 Francis gained the right to appoint France's bishops and abbots, another source for patronage. He centralized royal control into an inner council and asserted more strongly his legal powers (*lit de justice*). After Francis, the Reformation and civil wars reduced royal authority again.

8. United Spain

The marriage of Isabella of Castile and Ferdinand of Aragon in 1469 led to the union of these two powerful kingdoms in the Iberian peninsula.

9. Ferdinand and Isabella

By 1500 these monarchs had dramatically increased royal power in Spain. They reduced the power of the nobility, imposed law and order in Castile, acquired the dependence of lesser aristocrats (*hidalgos*), spread a centralized bureaucracy, gained authority over justice, drove Moors and Jews from the country, increased royal revenues, and employed the Inquisition to secure religious and political unity.

10. Foreign Affairs

Ferdinand extended his kingdom with diplomatic and military skill. With the most effective standing army of the age, Spain became a major power in Italy. Its diplomatic corps had no equal.

11. Charles V, Holy Roman Emperor

Charles inherited Spain and, as a Habsburg, was elected Holy Roman Emperor (1519). Initially, because Charles was not Spanish, there was much hostility in

Spain, which resulted in a number of revolts. Order was soon restored under the leadership of nobles, and a detailed Spanish administration was shaped by Francisco de los Cobos. Spain became a vast federation of territories controlled by departmental and territorial councils and powerful viceroys, with Castile at the heart of power. This allowed for some local flexibility, while giving the crown the power it wanted.

12. The Financial Toll of War

Almost ceaseless wars drained the Habsburgs and Spain financially. Much of this burden was supported by bullion from America and loans from Italian and German financiers, who monopolized most of Spain's trade with the New World. In 1557 the monarchy declared the first of a series of bankruptcies.

IV. The Splintered States

1. The Holy Roman Empire

Areas to the east of England, France, and Spain did not experience the same pattern of centralization. In the Holy Roman Empire, weak institutions prevented the emergence of strong central government. Most of these lands remained divided into numerous autonomous principalities, towns, and ecclesiastical units. The stronger princes continued to dominate most of these lands and the major central representative institution, the Diet.

2. Eastern Europe

In Eastern Europe, the Hungarian and Polish patterns of a loss of power by the monarch, a growth of authority by the nobility, and a revival of serfdom prevailed. However strong central authority was maintained in the Ottoman Empire.

3. Italy

In 1494 a series of wars between Italian states, leading to continual involvement of the French and Habsburgs, was initiated. By 1559 the Habsburgs controlled most of Italy, with the exception of Venice, Tuscany, and the Papal States. The small Italian political units were unable to survive onslaughts from large, centralized kingdoms.

V. The New Statecraft

1. International Relations

Italian states developed new ways of pursuing foreign policy that spread throughout Europe and constituted a revolution in diplomacy. They established resident ambassadors and developed the rudiments of a balance-of-power system.

2. Machiavelli and Guicciardini

Political commentators turned from arguments based on divine will or contractual law to those based on pragmatism, opportunism, and effective government to explain political events, especially in Italy. Machiavelli analyzed power. In *The Prince*, he told the ruler how to acquire and maintain power, recommending methods to inspire fear and respect when useful. In *Discourses*, he developed a cyclical theory of government and argued that healthy government depends on the willingness of all citizens to participate actively in civic life. Guicciardini (*History of Italy*) was the first major historian to rely heavily on original documents. He, like Machiavelli, was pessimistic about politics.

GUIDE TO DOCUMENTS

Two Views of Columbus

1. Compare the two views of Columbus. With whom do you most agree and why?
2. How do you explain the differences between these two views of Columbus? In what ways might a historian's times and attitudes affect what the historian writes?

Henry VIII Claims Independence from the Pope

1. How does Henry VIII justify monarchical power?
2. Why might this legal question be of such great historical significance?

SIGNIFICANT INDIVIDUALS

Explorers

Henry the Navigator (1394–1460), prince of Portugal, patron of explorers.

Vasco da Gama (1469?–1524), Portuguese, route around Africa to the East.

Christopher Columbus (1451–1506), Genoese, discoverer of America.

Ferdinand Magellan (1480–1521), Portuguese, circumnavigated the world.

Conquerors

Hernando Cortés (1485–1547), Spanish, conqueror of Mexico.

Francisco Pizarro (1470?–1541), Spanish, conqueror of Peru.

Political Leaders

Henry VII (1485–1509), first Tudor king of England.

Henry VIII (1509–1547), king of England

Cardinal Thomas Wolsey (1515–1529), chief minister of England.

Thomas Cromwell (1532–1540), chief minister of England.

Louis XI (1461–1483), king of France.

Charles VIII (1483–1498), king of France.

Francis I (1515–1547), king of France.

Isabella (1474–1504), queen of Castile.

Ferdinand (1479–1516), king of Aragon.

Charles V (1516–1556), king of Spain, (1519–1556), Holy Roman Emperor.

Matthias Corvinus (1458–1490), king of Hungary.

Cultural Figures

Niccolò Machiavelli (1469–1527), Italian political philosopher.

Francesco Guicciardini (1483–1520), Italian historian.

CHRONOLOGICAL DIAGRAM

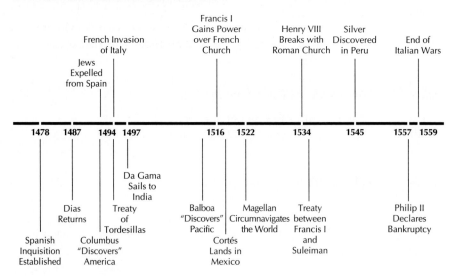

IDENTIFICATION

the commercial revolution
capitalism
viceroys
justices of the peace
the council (in Star Chamber)
Estates General
taille
standing army
sale of offices

"new monarch"
gentry
hidalgo
Moriscos
Diet
resident ambassador
balance of power
The Prince

MAP EXERCISES

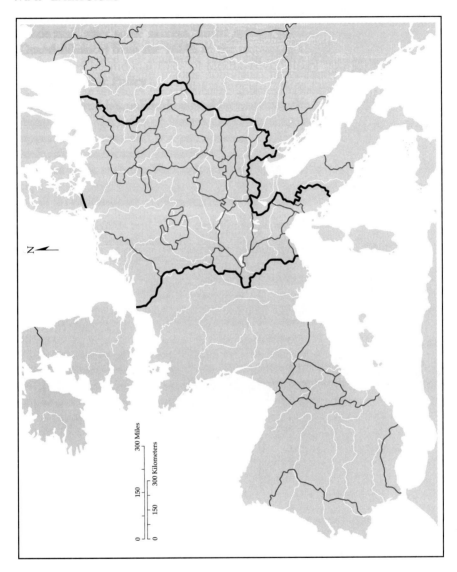

1. Label the *main* political divisions of Europe in the mid-sixteenth century.
2. Indicate the areas ruled by Charles V.

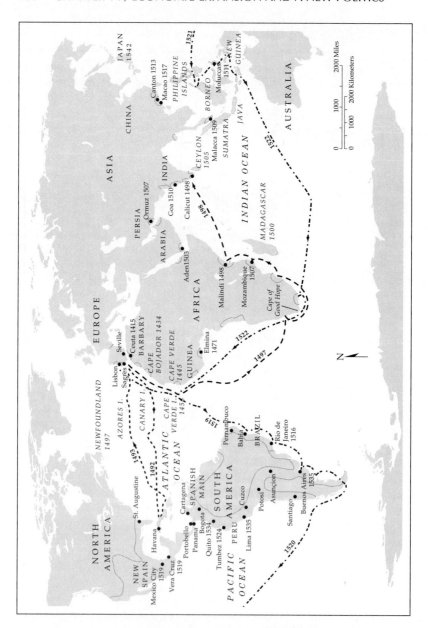

1. Label Portuguese possessions and Spanish possessions.
2. Indicate the routes taken by Columbus, Dias, da Gama, and Magellan and his crew.

PROBLEMS FOR ANALYSIS

I. *Expansion at Home*

1. What were some of the economic and social consequences of population increase?
2. What developments in prices, commerce, and industry evidenced economic growth? Why? What were the social consequences of this?

II. *Expansion Overseas*

1. What motivated the exploration and expansion?
2. Distinguish between the Portuguese and Spanish patterns of exploration and expansion. What part did the size of Spain and of fifteenth- and sixteenth-century political and military developments play in this difference?

III. *The Centralization of Political Power*

1. What developments and policies characterized the "new monarchies" of Western Europe?
2. Compare any two "new monarchies," focusing on the developments that distinguished the two, despite their similarities.

IV. *The Splintered States*

1. What is the historical significance of the failure of central authority to grow in Italy and much of Eastern Europe? Who became the holders of power in these areas? What were the consequences for the lower classes?

V. *The New Statecraft*

1. What distinguished diplomacy during the sixteenth century from that of previous time? Why did Italy play such an important role in this?
2. Machiavelli and Guicciardini were original observers of contemporary political events. What was so importantly new about their observations? In what ways did their observations reflect the events of their times?

SPECULATIONS

1. If Machiavelli were alive today, what kinds of recommendations would he make to someone who wanted to gain and retain political office?
2. If you were adviser to Charles V, what policies would you suggest to retain the wealth coming from South America within Spain? What factors would you have to consider in making your recommendations?
3. What do you think most motivated the explorers and conquerors? What kind of evidence would support your argument?

TRANSITIONS

In "Reformations in Religion," the religious revolutions that tore Europe apart during the sixteenth century were examined.

In "Economic Expansion and a New Politics," Europe experienced population and economic growth. Europe also expanded geographically throughout the world. These trends fit well with the establishment of powerful "new monarchies" in Western Europe. Lacking such strong, unifying central governments, the splintered states of the Holy Roman Empire, Italy, and much of Eastern Europe fell behind in the international struggle for power. The new statecraft developed in Italy and spread to the rest of Europe.

In "War and Crisis," the international and domestic upheaval between 1560 and 1660, inflamed by religious tensions, will be examined.

SECTION SUMMARY
TRANSITION, RENAISSANCE, AND REFORMATION
1300–1559
CHAPTERS 11–14

CHRONOLOGICAL DIAGRAM

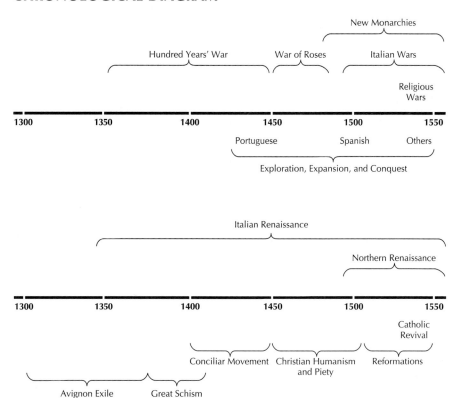

MAP EXERCISES

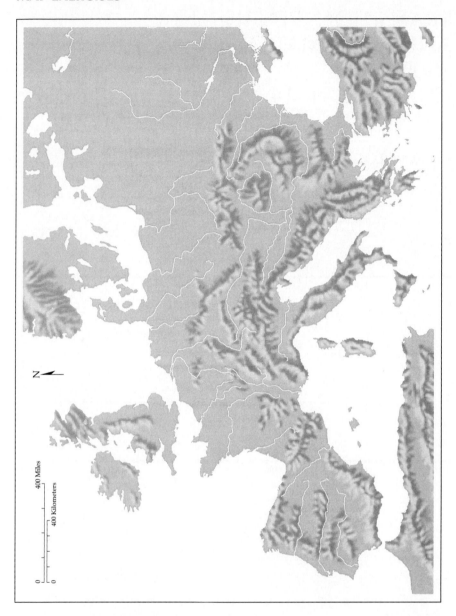

1. Indicate the following:
   a. The areas controlled by the various "new monarchies" and the approx-
      imate date of the establishment of the "new monarchies."
   b. The areas ruled by Charles V about 1550.
   c. Religious divisions about 1550.

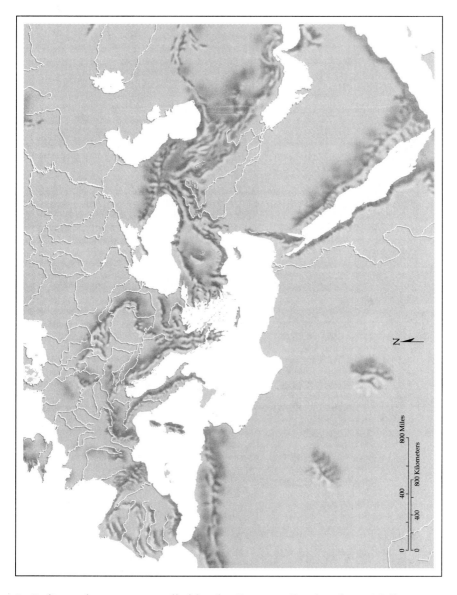

1. Indicate the areas controlled by the Ottoman Empire about 1560.

1. Indicate and label those areas of Europe expanding their control to non-Western areas of the world during the fifteenth and sixteenth centuries.
2. Indicate those areas of the non-Western world controlled by European powers by 1560.

BOX CHARTS

Reproduce the Box Charts in a larger format in your notebook or on separate sheets of paper.

Chart 1	England 1300 — 1559	France 1300 — 1559	Spain 1300 — 1559	Italy 1300 — 1559	Holy Roman Empire 1300 — 1559
Cultural Values and Productions					
Religious System and Characteristics					
Social System and Characteristics					
Economic System and Characteristics					
Political Institutions and Developments					

Chart 2

Europe

	1300	1350	1400	1450	1500	1559
Political Leaders						
Explorers and Conquerors						
Religious Leaders						
Humanists						
Philosophers						
Writers						
Painters						
	1300	1350	1400	1450	1500	1559

FIFTEEN
WAR AND CRISIS

MAIN THEMES

1. A series of costly, devastating wars, inflamed by religious motives, raged in Europe in the period between the 1560s and 1650s.
2. The most devastating war was the Thirty Years' War. It was brought to an end by the Peace of Westphalia, which signified major international changes and a new period of relative calm.
3. New weapons, tactics, and armies revolutionized war during the period.
4. Throughout Europe tensions created great internal unrest, often breaking out in revolt and civil war.
5. During the mid-seventeenth century, new political patterns were established that would hold for some time.

OUTLINE AND SUMMARY

I. *Wars of Religion in the Age of Philip II*

Religious conflict motivated warfare that plagued Europe between the 1560s and 1650s.

1. *The Crusades of Philip II*

Philip II ignited war in his successful struggles against the Muslims in the Mediterranean (battle of Lepanto) and his unsuccessful efforts in France and against the Dutch and English (the Armada, 1588).

2. *The Dutch Revolt*

In a protracted struggle, the independence-minded Dutch Calvinists united behind William of Orange in revolt against Philip II, eventually gaining their independence.

3. *Civil War in France*

After the death of Henry II in 1559, France became divided into two warring parties: the Catholics, led by the Guise family, and the Calvinists (Huguenots), led by the Bourbon family. Catherine de Medici, the real power behind the weak sons of Henry II, was unable to control the nobles led by these two families. The rise to power and conversion of the Bourbon Henry IV, the assassination of the duke of Guise, the weakening of the Catholics' main ally (Spain), and a weariness of war led to the defeat of the Catholic League. In 1598 the fighting ended, and Henry granted toleration to the Huguenots. These decades of strife influenced political thought. Both Huguenots and Catholics developed contractual theories of government to justify revolt against the king. Moderate political theorists (the *politiques*) such as Jean Bodin (*The Six Books of the Republic*) emphasized peace, unity, and national security through an equilibrium between control and freedom.

II. War and International Crises

1. The Thirty Years' War

Between 1618 and 1648 the Holy Roman Empire suffered through a series of encounters known as the Thirty Years' War. Initially religion was the chief issue, but politics and international affairs became entwined with and sometimes prevailed over religious issues. Between 1618 and 1630 the Catholic Habsburgs—led by Emperor Ferdinand, Maximilian of Bavaria, and Albrecht von Wallenstein—prevailed.

Intervention by Protestant Sweden, led by Gustavus Adolphus, and by France in the 1630s and 1640s turned the tide. In 1648 peace was achieved, but only after great loss of life (more than a third of Germany's population) and economic dislocation. Wars in the Spanish Netherlands and around the Baltic did not end until 1661.

2. The Peace of Westphalia

The Peace of Westphalia in 1648 was a landmark. For the first time, all participants came together at a peace conference and decided all outstanding issues. France and Sweden were the main winners; the Habsburgs, the main losers. France replaced Spain as the dominant continental power. Economic leadership shifted northward to England and the Netherlands. The settlement was regarded as the basis for all international negotiations for more than a century. After Westphalia, wars would continue—but for nonreligious purposes, at lesser human cost, and with more sense of control.

III. The Military Revolution

1. Weapons and Tactics

During the sixteenth and seventeenth century important changes in military equipment, tactics, and organization took place. Gunpowder came into general use. Sieges became more complicated and costly. The infantry, organized in huge squares, gained dominance over the cavalry. Standing armies grew in numbers and cost. Then Maurice of Nassau and Gustavus Adolphus developed new tactics emphasizing mobility and the salvo to counter the dominance of the Spanish infantry.

2. *The Organization and Support of Armies*

Increasingly large permanent professional armies caused a rapid growth of supporting administrative personnel, an increase in taxation, and a new opportunity for social mobility in the officer corps.

3. *The Life of the Soldier*

Men sometimes volunteered for military life; but sometimes they had to be tricked, pressured, or forced into the ranks. Though eventually paid, soldiers relied on local civilians for needs. Military justice was officially severe, but not so in fact. Disease and boredom were common companions.

IV. *Revolution in England*

During the 1640s and 1650s, revolts were common but revolution occurred only in England.

1. *Elizabeth I*

Little affected by war, unified by common bonds such as Parliament and Protestantism, England was relatively calm between the 1560s and the 1630s. Elizabeth I (1558–1603) was extraordinarily clever, strong, and popular. However, the power and wealth of the great nobles (some 60 in number) was declining relative to the rise of the gentry (some 20,000), who were benefiting from governmental service, agricultural wealth, increasing prices, and commercial investment. At the same time merchants led in England's commercial and industrial expansion. The gentry and merchants increasingly resented interference by Elizabeth's successors and sympathized with the dissenting Puritans.

2. *Parliament and the Law*

The gentry increased their influence and power through the House of Commons, which they controlled. They used their revenue powers and the common-law tradition to counter the policies of the financially pressed James I.

3. *Rising Antagonisms*

Under Charles I (1625–1649) conflict between Parliament, Puritans, common lawyers, and disenchanted country gentry on the one hand and the crown on the other intensified, leading Charles to rule without Parliament for 11 years. A religion-sparked invasion by the Scots required Charles to call on Parliament for help.

4. Civil War

Under the leadership of John Pym and Oliver Cromwell, Parliament asserted itself against the king and the Anglican Church (the Grand Remonstrance). A royalist party formed, the country divided, and the Civil War broke out. Divisions were unclear, but generally royalists were younger and from the rural north and west, while supporters of Parliament tended to be older, from the more cosmopolitan south and east, and allies of the Puritans. A small group of radical Puritans kept up the momentum. The antiroyalists, supported by the Scots, were at first successful. Then they split; the more radical Independents under the leadership of Oliver Cromwell and his New Model Army succeeded over the allied royalists, Scots, and Presbyterians in 1647. The remaining members of Parliament (the "Rump" Parliament) tried Charles, who continued to plot against them, and had him executed (1649).

5. England under Cromwell

Cromwell faced factions on all sides, including such groups as the egalitarian Levellers and Diggers. Unable to secure a new constitutional structure for government, he reluctantly took personal command in 1653. After his death in 1658 his son Richard took over but was not strong enough to prevail against General George Monck, who invited Charles II to power in 1660. Other than establishing the political power of the gentry, only relatively minor changes resulted from the revolution. The increased power of the gentry would be illustrated by the bloodless coup against the king in the 1680s.

V. Revolts in France and Spain

1. The France of Henry IV

By the time of his death in 1610 Henry IV had succeeded in reestablishing royal authority by manipulating the aristocracy and increasing his revenues through new sales of offices and an officeholder's fee (the *paulette*). The crown adopted a set of economic attitudes called mercantilism, making the government more responsible for commerce, industry, and the promotion of prosperity.

2. Louis XIII

Between 1610 and 1624 Marie de Medici and later the young Louis XIII managed to hold the weak monarchy together in the face of unrest of nobles and Calvinists. After 1624 the talented minister Cardinal Richelieu reasserted royal power. He utilized the powerful bureaucracy, undermined the nobility, increased the power of the *intendants,* and crushed the Huguenots at La Rochelle. Yet because of increasing taxes and resentful local nobles, France experienced a succession of peasant uprisings.

3. Political Crisis

Between 1648 and 1652 upper levels of French society—the nobles, townspeople, and members of parlements—struggled to wrest power from the monarchy (the Fronde). Despite temporary loses, the monarchy, led by Cardinal Mazarin, was victorious. The crown would be strong and stable for years.

4. Sources of Discontent in Spain

Disunity among Spain's vast domains, from the Low Countries to the New World, was Philip II's chief problem. Decisions came slowly, and the standing army proved costly. Philip's emphasis on the Catholic faith was popular within Spain. Economic problems mounted because Spain's New World treasure and lucrative domestic wool industry benefited only small groups, mostly foreigners. Overspending brought the crown to bankruptcy. Moreover Spain suffered a serious decline of population during the seventeenth century. These problems made Spain unable to support its renewed involvement in the Thirty Years' War.

5. Revolt and Secession

Reacting against the count of Olivares' program (the Union of Arms) to unify or "Castilianize" Spain, Catalonia, Portugal, Naples, and Sicily revolted in the 1640s. The great period of Spain's international domination was over as it became a stable second-level state run by its nobility.

VI. Political Change in an Age of Crisis

1. The United Provinces

The United Provinces were unique in several ways, above all by being more socially homogeneous and politically open than any other republic. The Dutch quickly gained economic mastery over European finance and trade (especially in Amsterdam). The wealth, openness, and religious tolerance of the Dutch supported an explosion of cultural creativity. Politically there was tension between the mercantile party, which dominated the Estates General, and the House of Orange. In times of peace, particularly under the leadership of Jan De Witt between 1653 and 1672, the more pacific and economically oriented mercantile party prevailed. In time of war, authority shifted to the centralizing House of Orange under such leaders as Maurice of Nassau, William II, and William III.

2. Sweden

Gustavus Adolphus (1611–1632) led Sweden from a second-rate position to dominance in northern Europe. He unified the nobles, organized an efficient bureaucracy, and led a powerful army. Sweden's economy gained strength. After his death, the nobles gained power. In 1650, Queen Christina—with the help of townspeople, peasants, and the Riksdag (assembly)—restrained the nobles. Under Charles X power gradually shifted away from the great nobles.

3. Eastern Europe and the "Crisis"

Limits to Ottoman rule were confirmed, Poland's central government was weakened, and Russia's central government began consolidating its power.

GUIDE TO DOCUMENTS

Queen Elizabeth's Armada Speech

1. How does Elizabeth attempt to appeal to the troops?
2. In what ways does she justify her own political power?

Oliver Cromwell's Aims

1. What are Cromwell's reasons for declining the offer to serve as king?
2. How does Cromwell's reasoning reflect his religious beliefs and the role religion played in the civil war?

Richelieu on Diplomacy

1. In what ways does this excerpt reflect the connections between diplomacy and international interests of the state during this period?
2. How might this attitude help explain Richelieu's extraordinary success?

SIGNIFICANT INDIVIDUALS

Political and Military Leaders

Elizabeth I (1558–1603), queen of England.

James I (1603–1625), king of England.

Charles I (1625–1649), king of England.

John Pym (1584–1643), English parliamentary leader.

Oliver Cromwell (1599–1658), English revolutionary, lord protector.

Catherine de Medici (1519–1589), regent and power in France.

Duke of Guise (1550–1588), powerful French Catholic noble.

Henry IV (1589–1610), king of France.

Louis XIII (1610–1643), king of France.

Gustavus Adolphus (1611–1632), king of Sweden.

Ferdinand II (1619–1637), Holy Roman Emperor.

Cardinal Richelieu (1624–1642), chief minister in France.

Cardinal Mazarin (1642–1661), chief minister in France.

Philip II (1556–1598), king of Spain.

Duke of Alva (1508–1583), Spanish general.

Philip III (1598–1621), king of Spain.

Philip IV (1621–1665), king of Spain.

Count of Olivares (1621–1643), chief minister of Spain.

William of Orange (1533–1584), Dutch leader.

Maurice of Nassau (1587–1625), Dutch leader

Jan De Witt (1625–1672), Dutch statesman.

Albrecht von Wallenstein (1583–1634), imperial general.

Political Theorists

Jean Bodin (1530–1596), French
   politique.

CHRONOLOGICAL DIAGRAM

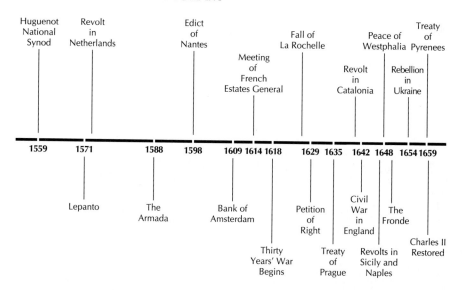

IDENTIFICATION

the salvo
the Armada
the Catholic League
Edict of Nantes
Huguenots
politiques
Peace of Westphalia
the gentry

Grand Remonstrance
New Model Army
"Rump" Parliament
Levellers
the *paulette*
mercantilism
the Fronde
Union of Arms

MAP EXERCISES

1. Indicate those areas under the rule of Philip II of Spain. What does this reveal about some of the problems facing him.
2. Indicate areas of Protestant resistance to the religious policies of Philip II.

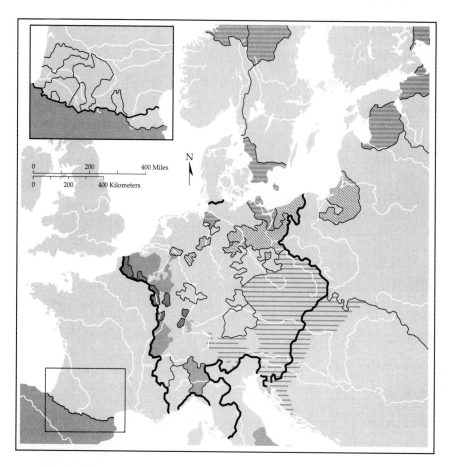

1. Indicate the lands controlled by the Austrian Habsburgs, the Spanish Habsburgs, France, Brandenburg-Prussia, and Sweden in 1660.

PROBLEMS FOR ANALYSIS

I. Wars of Religion in the Age of Philip II

1. Evaluate the relative weight of religious and political factors underlying the wars between the 1560s and 1640s.
2. What problems faced Philip II?

II. War and International Crisis

1. In what ways does the Thirty Years' War reflect the mixture of politics and religion in war during this period?
2. What was the significance of the Peace of Westphalia?

III. The Military Revolution

1. What changes in military equipment, tactics, and organization took place during the sixteenth and seventeenth centuries? What were some of the economic, social, and political consequences of these changes?

IV. Revolution in England

1. How do you explain the civil war and revolution in England? Were opponents clearly split along religious or social lines?
2. What role did Cromwell play during this period?

V. Revolts in France and Spain

1. Compare the issues that caused discord in France and England. Is it fair to consider the Fronde similar to the English revolution? Why?
2. How do you explain Spain's decline in the seventeenth century? Evaluate the role economic factors played in this decline.

VI. Political Change in an Age of Crisis

1. What was so unusual about the United Provinces? How would you explain its rapid economic and cultural success?
2. How was Sweden able to rise from a second-rate power to a position of dominance in the Baltic during the seventeenth century? What policies did Gustavus Adolphus follow to this end?
3. Compare the general nature of constitutional settlements reached throughout Europe at midcentury. In what areas did monarchical power prevail? In what areas was monarchical power weakened?

SPECULATIONS

1. How might Charles I have prevented the English Civil War and revolution?
2. As a political leader in the early seventeenth century, would you use religion for your own ends? What are the dangers in doing or not doing this?
3. As adviser to Philip II of Spain, what policies would you recommend to prevent the eventual decline of Spanish power? Why?

TRANSITIONS

In "Economic Expansion and a New Politics," the economic advances during the late-fifteenth century and the sixteenth century, the process of European expansion, and the growth of political authority around the "new monarchs" of Western Europe were examined.

In "War and Crisis," we see the period between the 1560s and 1650s dominated by war and internal revolt. Politics and religion entwined in these upheavals, above all in the civil wars in England and France and the Thirty Years' War in the Holy Roman Empire. The period ends with a relative sense of constitutional and military stability in most places, which was to last for some time.

In "Culture and Society in the Age of the Scientific Revolution," the social, cultural, and intellectual patterns paralleling these political and international trends during the sixteenth and seventeenth centuries will be explored.

SIXTEEN
CULTURE AND SOCIETY
IN THE AGE OF THE
SCIENTIFIC REVOLUTION

MAIN THEMES

1. A small number of thinkers overturned accepted ideas about nature and laid the foundations for modern science in the period from the mid-sixteenth to the mid-seventeenth century.
2. Major breakthroughs in physics, astronomy, mathematics, and anatomy rested on the new scientific principles of reason, doubt, observation, generalization, and testing by experiment.
3. Cultural styles evolved, from the distortion of Mannerism to the drama of the Baroque and the discipline of Classicism.
4. Seventeenth-century society was hierarchical, with mobility increasingly common in the higher orders but a rarity for the lower orders.
5. The traditional village was changing and being pulled into the activities of the territorial state.
6. General attitudes were marked by beliefs in magic and mystical forces.

OUTLINE AND SUMMARY

I. *The Scientific Revolution*

   1. *Origins of the Scientific Revolution*

A number of factors supported the scientific revolution. Accepted theories of ancient Greek scholars—such as Aristotle in physics, Ptolemy in astronomy, and Galen in medicine—did not cover all the facts. Other Greek writings were discovered that indicated disagreement. Various "magical" beliefs, such as alchemy, reflected a growing view that there were simple, comprehensive keys to nature. A belief in the importance of careful measurement and observation had been growing, as illustrated by the invention of such instruments as the telescope, thermometer, barometer, and microscope; these combined to support a new scientific approach pioneered by Francis Bacon.

   2. *The Breakthroughs*

In 1543 Vesalius (*The Structure of the Human Body*) published important advances in anatomy. In that same year Copernicus (*On the Revolutions of the Heavenly Spheres*) published a mathematically sophisticated theory of planetary movement, placing the sun rather than the earth at the center of the universe. Tycho Brahe made important astronomical observations. A sense of scholarly uncertainty was growing.

3. Kepler and Galileo

Relying on mathematics, Kepler discovered three laws of planetary motion (1609–1619) that were revolutionary and of fundamental importance. Galileo combined mathematics, technical observation, and logic to reveal major new discoveries. He confirmed the earth as simply another revolving body, subject to the same laws of motion as the rest of the universe. He proposed the principle of inertia to explain all motion. He argued that every physical law is equally applicable throughout the universe. His rejection of authority and the argument that the earth moved (*Dialogue on the Two Great World Systems,* 1632) caused the famous condemnation by the Inquisition in 1633. By midcentury the new findings in physics, astronomy, and anatomy (enlarged by Harvey's discovery that the blood circulates) created a new, influential kind of certainty.

4. Isaac Newton

The versatile Newton united physics and astronomy in a single system to explain motion throughout the universe; he helped transform mathematics by the development of calculus and established some of the basic laws of modern physics. Newton represented the power of mathematics and experimentation against the methods of Descartes. His masterpiece was the *Principia* (1687); his most dramatic findings, the three laws of motion. He saw the universe as a system of impersonal, uniform forces—a vast, stable machine. Newton dominated physics and astronomy and became a powerful intellectual symbol.

5. A New Epistemology

Scientists moved toward a new theory of how to obtain and verify knowledge —a theory that was based on experience, reason, and doubt, rather than on authority. After formulation of a hypothesis, the process had three parts: observation, generalization, and testing. The language of science was mathematics.

6. The Wider Influence of Scientific Thought

Propagandizers helped spread acceptance of scientific methods.

7. Bacon and Descartes

Francis Bacon was the greatest of these propagandizers, picturing scientific research as a collective enterprise gathering information that would lead to practical universal laws (*New Atlantis,* 1627), René Descartes applied the scientific method of doubt to all knowledge, relying on logical thought rather than on authority or the senses (*Discourse on Method,* 1637). He made an influential distinction between spirit and matter, and helped create *mechanism,* viewing the universe as a complicated machine.

8.   Blaise Pascal

A brilliant mathematician and experimenter, Pascal became influenced by Jansenism, a pious form of Catholicism that emphasized human weakness. He argued (*Pensées*) that scientific truths were less important than religious truths, a unique protest.

9.   Science Institutionalized

A number of scientific societies, such as the Royal Society (London, 1660) and the Royal Academy of Sciences (France, 1666), were established as headquarters and clearing centers for research. Supported by royal patronage, these societies published scientific journals (*Philosophical Transactions,* 1665) and helped elevate their members in prestige. The understanding and the sense of order, harmony, and reason that science was creating spread widely.

II.   Literature and the Arts

Changes in culture paralleled the evolution from disorder to order in other areas.

1.   Mannerism

Mannerist painters such as El Greco reacted to the upheavals of the sixteenth century by attempting to escape reality through distortion.

2.   Michel de Montaigne

The humanist and philosopher Montaigne created the essay form. He emphasized Skepticism and the search for self-knowledge. He reflected a broader *Neostoicism,* as did Justus Lipsius.

3.   Cervantes and Shakespeare

Cervantes captured the disillusionment accompanying Spain's decline in his novel *Don Quixote.* He satirized the chivalry of the nobles while portraying the often hypocritical lives of ordinary people. His contemporary William Shakespeare was the greatest creative artist of the English-speaking world. In his plays Shakespeare reflects not only the tensions of his own times but the timeless human problems of love, hatred, violence, and morality.

4.   The Baroque: Grandeur and Excitement

After 1600 the Baroque—emphasizing passion, drama, mystery, and awe—gained prominence in the arts. Flourishing mostly in Rome and at the leading Catholic courts in Munich, Prague, Madrid, and Brussels, the Baroque is best exemplified by the powerful paintings of Caravaggio, the grandiose paintings of Rubens, the court paintings of Velázquez, and the elaborate sculpture and architecture of Bernini. In music, new instruments (keyboard and string families), new forms (the opera), and the orchestra were developed, above all by Claudio Monteverdi (*Orfeo*, 1607).

5. Classicism: Grandeur and Restraint

The Classical style of the seventeenth century aimed at grandiose effects—but through restraint and discipline, and within the bounds of formal structure. This style, as exemplified by subdued scenes of Poussin and the dignified portraits of Dutch painters such as Rembrandt, echoes the broad trend towards stabilization. By the middle of the seventeenth century the Classical style spread to literature; examples are the dramas of Corneille (*Le Cid*, 1636) and Racine.

III. Social Patterns and Popular Culture

1. Population Trends

Population decline marked the first half of the seventeenth century. People usually married late, died young, and could expect only one out of two children to reach adulthood. Famine, poor nutrition, disease, and war directly affected population growth, which eventually stabilized and grew slightly during the second half of the century.

2. Social Status

Although seventeenth-century society was supposedly composed of relatively fixed ranks and orders, wealth and education were gaining in social importance, indicating that mobility to desirable positions of prestige and privilege was occurring. High status conferred a variety of privileges. Women were generally considered subordinate to men.

3. Mobility and Crime

Mobility was a rarity for the lower levels of society. Some peasants were able to avoid the increased taxes, rising rents, and additional demands of the late sixteenth century by escaping to the cities or into the army; but poor wages, crime, and an early death were commonly their fate.

4. Change in the Village

The traditional village in the West was changing from a closed, self-sufficient, and cohesive unit. Agricultural changes increased differences in wealth, royal officials intruded in local affairs, and nobles stayed away—attracted to central courts and yet demanding more from their villages.

5. City Life

Cities grew, offering some opportunity and linking villages to the national market.

6. *Popular Culture in the City*

With the growth of literacy came more newspapers, coffeehouses, theater, and books.

7. *Magic and Rituals*

People generally believed that mysterious forces controlled nature and their lives. The world was occupied by powerful spirits, both good and evil. These assumptions found expression in special processions, holidays, violent demonstrations (often led by women), and peasant uprisings. There was widespread belief in magic.

8. *Witchcraft*

The great witch craze of the sixteenth and seventeenth centuries, reflecting the notion that misfortunes must have been willed by someone, resulted in thousands of deaths—particularly among women.

9. *Forces of Restraint*

The assault on witches faded away toward the end of the century. Urbanization contributed to a general drift away from magical beliefs as did better-educated religious authorities.

GUIDE TO DOCUMENTS

Galileo and Kepler on Copernicus

1. What might be the restraints on the development and spread of new ideas reflected in these excerpts?
2. What does this reveal about the potential strength of the new scientific community in Europe?

A Witness Analyzes the Witch Craze

1. According to Linden, what were the motives for the witch-hunts?
2. What were some of the forces that led to the decline of the witch-hunts?

SIGNIFICANT INDIVIDUALS

Scientists

Andreas Vesalius (1514–1564), Belgian anatomist.

Nicolaus Copernicus (1473–1543), Polish astronomer.

Johannes Kepler (1571–1630), German astronomer.

Galileo Galilei (1564–1643), Italian astronomer, physicist.

William Harvey (1578–1657),
English anatomist.

Isaac Newton (1642–1727), English
astronomer, physicist,
mathematician.

Philosophers

Francis Bacon (1561–1626),
English philosopher.
René Descartes (1596–1650), French
philosopher, mathematician.

Thomas Hobbes (1588–1679),
English political theorist.
Blaise Pascal (1623–1662), French
mathematician, experimenter.

Mannerists

El Greco (1548?–1625?),
Greek-Spanish painter.

Baroque

Peter Paul Rubens (1577–1640),
Flemish painter.
Diego Velázquez (1599–1660),
Spanish painter.
Giovanni Lorenzo Bernini (1598–
1680), Italian sculptor, architect.

Rembrandt van Rijn (1606–1669),
Dutch painter.
Claudio Monteverdi (1567–1643),
Italian composer.

Classicism

Nicholas Poussin (1594–1665),
French painter.
Pierre Corneille (1606–1684),
French dramatist.

Jean Racine (1639–1699), French
dramatist.

Writers

Michel de Montaigne (1533–1592),
French essayist.
Miguel de Cervantes (1547–1616),
Spanish novelist.

William Shakespeare (1564–1616),
English dramatist, poet.

CHRONOLOGICAL DIAGRAM

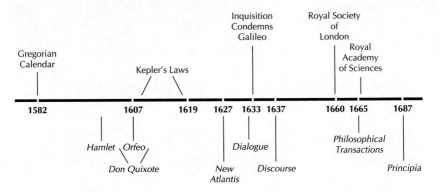

IDENTIFICATION

alchemy
scientific method
three laws of motion
mechanism
Skepticism
seigneurial reaction

Jansenism
Royal Society of London
Philosophical Transactions
Principia
great witch craze
Baroque

MAP EXERCISE

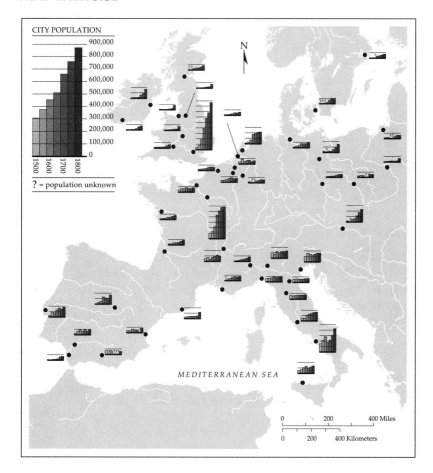

1. Label the five cities that grew most rapidly between 1500 and 1800.
2. Indicate and label Europe's eight largest cities in 1700.

PROBLEMS FOR ANALYSIS

I. *The Scientific Revolution*

1. Explain the origins of the scientific revolution. Were the theories of the ancient Greeks a hindrance or a support? What role did magical beliefs play?
2. What was the essence of the conflict between Galileo and the Church? Do you think it was in the Church's interest to condemn Galileo? Why?
3. Use examples to demonstrate the principles of the scientific method. How does the scientific method differ from earlier methods of obtaining and verifying knowledge?
4. Compare the methods emphasized by Francis Bacon, René Descartes, and Isaac Newton. Do you think that Blaise Pascal would disagree with the methods and concerns of these men? Why?

II. *Literature and the Arts*

1. Compare the Baroque and Classical styles. In what ways did they reflect other developments in sixteenth- and seventeenth-century Europe?
2. It has been argued that Cervantes and Shakespeare reflected the historical concerns of their own societies as well as timeless human concerns. Use examples to support this argument.

III. *Social Patterns and Popular Culture*

1. How was seventeenth-century society organized? Compare the possibilities for social mobility among various social groups.
2. What were some of the demographic characteristics of seventeenth-century society? How do you explain population patterns in the seventeenth century?
3. How did popular culture reflect a dependence on nature and the conditions of life among the peasantry? How does the great witch craze fit into this situation?
4. What were the causes for change in the traditional village? Were most of these causes internal, or were they a result of intrusions from the outside?

SPECULATIONS

1. The scientific revolution profoundly changed the ways in which people thought. It was difficult for many to accept this change. Today scientific ways of thinking are as accepted and taken for granted as traditional ways of thinking in the sixteenth century. What might a future change in the ways of thinking be like, and do you think such ways of thinking would be accepted without too much difficulty?
2. What would a debate between Galileo and the head of the Inquisition be like?

3. Are there any parallels between the great witch craze of the seventeenth century and more recent historical occurrences? Explain.

TRANSITIONS

In "War and Crisis," a period of violence and upheaval marked by unusually brutal warfare was examined. It was not until the mid-seventeenth century that the violence subsided and a new sense of order was attained.

In "Culture and Society in the Age of the Scientific Revolution," cultural and social patterns are shown to reflect this progression from uncertainty to stable resolution. This is clearest in the triumph of the scientific revolution—the revolutionary discoveries of a handful of men who laid the foundations for modern science—but it is also apparent in the evolution from Mannerism to the Classical style and in the increased control over people's lives gained by central governments. The upper classes throughout Europe benefited most from these trends.

In "The Emergence of the European State System," the course of political history during the second half of the seventeenth century will be explored. In this period absolutist kings continue the process of state building within a European society dominated by the aristocracy.

SEVENTEEN
THE EMERGENCE
OF THE EUROPEAN
STATE SYSTEM

MAIN THEMES

1. Louis XIV—by making his court at Versailles the center of society and by building the state's power through financial, domestic, and military policies —epitomized the absolutist monarchs of the late seventeenth century.
2. In related ways, absolutism grew in Austria, Prussia, and Russia.
3. The governments of England, the United Provinces, Sweden, and Poland were dominated by aristocrats or merchants. With the exception of England, these countries suffered a decline in power and influence.
4. Prussia, Austria, and England pursued state-building policies.
5. During the eighteenth century the states of Europe competed for authority and prestige, but within a system that created a balance of power.

OUTLINE AND SUMMARY

I. *The Creation of Absolutism in France*

1. *Versailles*

Absolutist monarchs made their great courts the center of society and royal culture. Louis XIV (1643–1715) built his elaborate court at Versailles and used it to impress the world and help domesticate the nobility. He justified his supremacy by emphasizing the divine right of kings to rule. In Paris, women established influential salons.

2. *Government*

Louis built the state's power by winning control over the use of armed force, the formulation and execution of laws, and the collection and expenditure of revenue. Control over the increasingly trained bureaucracy was crucial to this endeavor. His two leading ministers, Colbert in finance and Louvois in war, influenced Louis to pursue mercantilist economic policies and strengthen the army and border fortifications.

3. Foreign Policy

Louis followed a policy of expansion and dominance, but he failed against the Dutch and, after some success, failed against various combinations of allies (Grand Alliance) from the 1680s to the treaties of Utrecht (1713–1714).

4. Domestic Policy

Louis furthered his political control by revoking the toleration granted to the Huguenots in the Edict of Nantes (1685) and by suppressing Jansenism. He suppressed protests and peasant uprisings. Economically, Louis and Colbert made efforts to stimulate manufacturing, agriculture, and trade. Luxury industries and trade with the West Indies gained most.

5. The Condition of France

The famines (1690s and 1709) and the wars were costly, particularly for the lower classes. Nevertheless, the eighteenth century would witness an end to cycles of famine and plague and a greater concern of government for its people.

6. France after Louis XIV

After the death of Louis XIV, French kings faced renewed competition from aristocrats (especially in the parlements), financial instability (thanks to exemptions from taxes enjoyed by the privileged), and political weakness. Cardinal Fleury renewed royal authority between 1726 and 1743. Thereafter the weakness of the kings and conflicts with privileged groups created problems for the crown. Nevertheless, the eighteenth century was a period of relative growth and prosperity.

II. The Creation of Absolutism outside of France

1. The Habsburgs at Vienna

To a lesser degree, the Habsburg Leopold I (1658–1705) followed the pattern set at Versailles in his own court at Vienna (Schönbrunn). Relying on a small number of aristocrats in the Privy Council, he governed the lands with caution. At the urgings of Prince Eugène, he laid the foundations for the Austro-Hungarian Empire to the east. The nobility retained considerable local power.

2. The Habsburgs at Madrid

Spain declined rapidly, losing control over many lands outside the Iberian peninsula, and internally the nobles gained considerable autonomy.

3. The Hohenzollerns at Berlin

By allying himself with the nobles, creating a strong army, and organizing his country to support the military, elector Frederick William (1640–1688) built

Brandenburg-Prussia into the dominant principality in northern Germany. The Prussian landed nobility (Junkers) reimposed serfdom and made their estates profitable. His son, Frederick, took the title of king of Prussia in 1701 and made Berlin a focus of society and an intellectual and artistic center.

4. Peter the Great at St. Petersburg

Peter I (1682–1725) built an entirely new capital, St. Petersburg. He increased his power by taking over the Russian Orthodox Church and by ignoring representative institutions (the Duma). He simplified Russia's social order by reducing peasants and serfs to near uniformity under the heel of a single class of nobles. The aristocracy was made into a service class, required to hold positions in the bureaucracy. Whenever necessary, he imported experts from the West. By the end of his reign, Russia had expanded to dominance in the Baltic and was highly regarded throughout Europe.

III. Alternatives to Absolutism

1. The Triumph of the Gentry in England

Other late-seventeenth-century governments were dominated by aristocrats or merchants. The gentry—supported by custom, law, the House of Commons, and the results of the Civil War—was independently powerful in England. Charles II (1660–1685) managed to rule England effectively, but when his son, James II, encouraged Catholicism against the wishes of Parliament, leading members of the gentry invited William III to invade the country. James fled, and William and Mary were proclaimed monarchs in 1689. William ruled authoritatively but with clear limitations (the Bill of Rights, the Act of Toleration).

2. Politics and Prosperity

A small elite controlled the country's policy and institutions. This elite became divided into two parties: the Whigs, usually in power, and the Tories. England prospered economically, as evidenced by the success of the Bank of England (1694), the rise of the navy, and the overseas expansion. Though the prime beneficiaries were the gentry, even the lower classes improved their lot.

3. Aristocracy in the United Provinces, Sweden, and Poland

The Dutch republic fell increasingly under the power of the merchant oligarchy and provincial leadership in the Estates General. This elite was more restrained, egalitarian, and oriented toward economic goals than other elites in Europe. In the face of English competition, Dutch power declined in the eighteenth century. Initially Swedish kings continued the tradition of absolutism; but military defeats in the early eighteenth century resulted in the loss of Sweden's Baltic empire, and a resurgent nobility created a system, similar to England's, that gave them political and social power. Poland suffered from continued dominance of the old landed aristocracy, which eventually resulted in the dismemberment of this decentralized state in the late eighteenth century.

4. Contrasts in Political Thought

Imitating scientific methods, Hobbes constructed an original political theory from a few limited premises about human nature (*Leviathan,* 1651). He argued that people, inherently selfish and ambitious, remove themselves from a warlike state of nature by social contract to a peaceful society dominated by a sovereign power. Locke argued that we are born with the mind a clean slate (*tabula rasa*) and gain understanding by reasoning with data derived from the senses. He applied these principles to politics, systematizing the views of the English gentry (*Second Treatise of Civil Government,* 1690). Locke used Hobbes's notion of the creation of a sovereign power through a social contract ending the state of nature, but he reserved the rights of life, liberty, and property to the individual. His emphasis on property made him a spokesman for the elite.

IV. The State in the Eighteenth Century

1. State Building

Rival powers worked to strengthen their states internally, stressing military and economic power. This is illustrated by the development of Prussia and Austria.

2. The Prussia of Frederick William I

The spartan Frederick William I (1713–1740) increased the size of the army and improved the quality of its officers, instituted compulsory education, and unified administrative functions.

3. Frederick the Great

Although Frederick II (1740–1786) was a more cultured man than his father, he pursued with vigor Prussian state building through territorial acquisition. Gaining a reputation as an "enlightened" absolutist, he justified the monarch as the first servant of the state, and he pursued policies of religious toleration and judicial reform; yet he initiated his rule with a war to take Silesia from the Habsburgs.

4. The Habsburg Empire under Attack

The Habsburgs, attempting to centralize control over their dynastic holdings, faced strong opposition from local diets, different ethnic groups, and regional traditions. Charles VI's Pragmatic Sanction failed to secure Maria Theresa's claim to the Habsburg dominions; Prussia, France, Spain, and Bavaria attacked in the War of the Austrian Succession. With Hungarian troops and British gold,

Austria protected all but Silesia, which fell to Prussia. This outcome established Austria and Prussia as great rivals in Central Europe.

5. Maria Theresa

Though she was concerned with traditional religious and dynastic matters, Maria Theresa proved to be an innovative state builder. She improved Austria's tax base, instituted administrative reforms, and modernized the army.

6. The Growth of Stability in Great Britain

Britain expanded its government and international power. Parliament was dominant, controlled by an elite of landowners and leading townsmen. Though there were loose party alignments (Whigs and Tories), politics was largely controlled by small factions competing for patronage and offices. Britain created a bureaucratized state with a standing army and expanding navy; the cost was shared by the wealthy classes. The poor, however, suffered; and crime was endemic. Royal authority diminished under the Hanoverians George I and II, leaving more power in the hands of Parliament and key ministers such as Sir Robert Walpole. William Pitt, supported by London merchants and businessmen, opposed the relatively timid commercial and colonial policies of the government and eventually rose to power in 1758.

V. The International System

Effort was made to create a more impersonal and organized structure for diplomacy and warfare.

1. Diplomacy and Warfare

While dynastic interests remained important, they gave way to more impersonal considerations of state. To gain security and prosperity, any means were justified. An aristocratic, cosmopolitan, French-speaking corps of professional diplomats grew to maturity throughout Europe. Major powers dictated terms to the weaker states, as seen in the partitions of Poland.

2. Armies

Armies were large, disciplined, and costly. In war, maneuvering and organization became more important than brutality. Relative incompetence among the officer corps and the weakness of ties between allies further limited the actual scale of war.

3. The Seven Years' War

Austria achieved a diplomatic revolution by allying France and Russia against Prussia and England. Prussia attacked in 1756. Military might combined with the death of Empress Elizabeth of Russia and good fortune in diplomacy to save Frederick II. The Peace of Hubertusburg (1763) restored the status quo.

GUIDE TO DOCUMENTS

Louis XIV on Kingship

1. How does Louis XIV justify monarchical authority?
2. According to Louis XIV, in what ways should the monarch act?

Locke on the Origins of Government

1. According to Locke, why do men exit the state of nature and form a society with a government?
2. What, according to Locke, are the limits of society's power over the individual?

Maria Theresa in Vehement Mood

1. How does Maria Theresa justify her diplomatic realignment?
2. What, according to Maria Theresa, are Austria's proper reasons of state?

SIGNIFICANT INDIVIDUALS

Political Leaders

Louis XIV (1643–1715), king of France.
Louis XV (1715–1774), king of France.
Louis XVI (1774–1792), king of France.
Peter I (1682–1725), tsar of Russia.
Charles II (1660–1685), king of England.
Frederick William (1640–1688), elector of Brandenburg.
Frederick III, elector of Brandenburg (1688–1701) and first king of Prussia under the name and title of King Frederick I (1701–1713).

Frederick II (1740–1786), king of Prussia.
Maria Theresa (1740–1780), Austrian Habsburg monarch.
George I (1714–1727), king of England.
George II (1727–1760), king of England.
William III (1672–1702), stadholder of Holland (1689–1702), king of England.
Charles XI (1660–1697), king of Sweden.
Charles XII (1697–1718), king of Sweden.

Ministers and Generals

Jean-Baptiste Colbert (1619–1683), French financial reformer.
Marquis of Louvois (1641–1691), French minister of war.

Prince Eugène of Savoy (1663–1736), Austrian general and minister.
Cardinal Fleury (1720–1740), chief adviser to Louis XV.

Robert Walpole (1721–1742),
English prime minister.

William Pitt (1708–1778), English
statesman.

Political Theorists

Thomas Hobbes (1588–1679).

John Locke (1632–1704), English.

CHRONOLOGICAL DIAGRAM

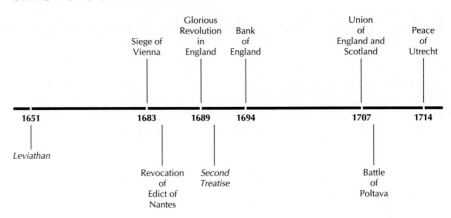

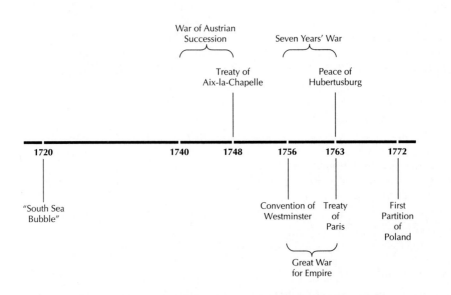

IDENTIFICATION

Grand Alliance
Peace of Utrecht
Whigs
Tories
Schönbrunn
Junkers
Bill of Rights
the salon
tabula rasa

balance of power
reasons of state
canton system
Pragmatic Sanction
aristocratic reaction
vingtième
"rotten" boroughs
diplomatic revolution

MAP EXERCISE

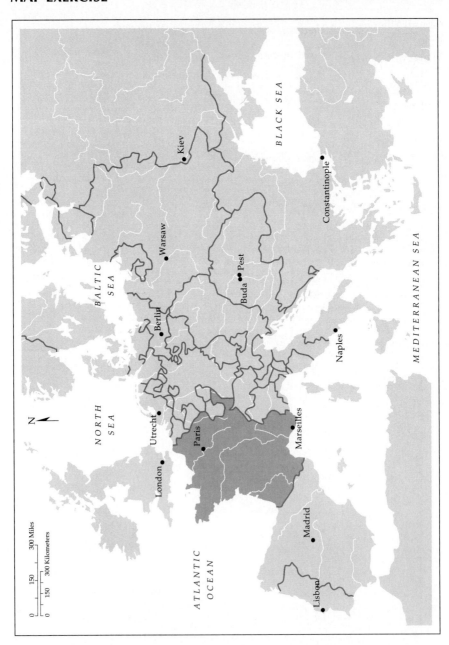

1. Label the main countries and empires in Europe in 1715.
2. Indicate areas where Louis XIV made efforts to expand France.

PROBLEMS FOR ANALYSIS

I. *The Creation of Absolutism in France*

1. In what ways did the policies of Louis XIV build the state's power? What evidences success or failure of these policies?

II. *The Creation of Absolutism outside of France*

1. How did the various absolutist monarchs pursue policies to support their own power while undermining that of their nobility?

III. *Alternatives to Absolutism*

1. What developments support the argument that during the late seventeenth century the gentry triumphed in England?
2. Compare the decentralization of government and society that occurred in the United Provinces, Sweden, and Poland during the late seventeenth and early eighteenth centuries.

IV. *The State in the Eighteenth Century*

1. Explain the relative success of Prussia during the eighteenth century.
2. How did Austria centralize state power during this period?

V. *The International System*

1. Compare the nature of war and diplomacy during the eighteenth century with that of the seventeenth century.
2. What role did "reasons of state" and dynastic interests play in the wars, diplomacy, and internal policies of European states during the eighteenth century? Give examples.

SPECULATIONS

1. First as an aristocrat, and second as a merchant, what were the advantages and disadvantages of living in a country dominated by an absolutist monarch?
2. How might Hobbes and Locke disagree with each other?
3. How might Machiavelli view political, diplomatic, and military developments during the eighteenth century? How might Hobbes?

TRANSITIONS

In "Culture and Society in the Age of the Scientific Revolution," the fundamental scientific discoveries and the cultural creations of this period were examined. These achievements contributed to a sense of order by the mid-seventeenth century.

In "The Emergence of the European State System," the quest for order remained the underlying concern throughout Europe. Absolutist kings, epitomized by Louis XIV, rose to prominence. With the exception of England, those states that failed to focus power on the monarch declined. The aristocracy, to varying degrees, dominated the new, powerful governmental administration as needed allies and agents of absolute monarchs or as direct controllers of events. During the eighteenth century international competition was reflected in efforts to further build the state internally.

In "The Wealth of Nations," the new social and economic developments as well as the development of eighteenth-century empires will be examined.